Basques Grouper takes his job as the head enforcer for the Maven coven very seriously. When his coven's Master Krispin learns that the nearby gargoyle clutch has a new chieftain, Basques is sent with his coven's second-in-command and another enforcer to meet with him. The meeting is going well . . . until a small blue gargoyle enters to serve refreshments, and Basques scents his blood. When he asks to taste the male, his over-eager approach, sends the gargoyle running. Basques learns the small gargoyle is Dloben, and under the prior chieftain's rule, he'd been abused. Working to change his approach, Basques must put his faith in the mate-pull and the advice of strangers. Can Basques convince his shy beloved that he's not like the dominant paranormals he's dealt with in the past?

A Vampire for his Own
Copyright © 2019 Charlie Richards
ISBN: 978-1-4874-2488-6
Cover art by Angela Waters

Published by eXtasy Books Inc or
Devine Destinies, an imprint of eXtasy Books Inc

Look for us online at:
www.eXtasybooks.com or www.devinedestinies.com

A Vampire for his Own
A Paranormal's Love: Book Twenty-Seven

By

Charlie Richards

DEDICATION

Nothing is so strong as gentleness. Nothing is so gentle as real strength.
~Ralph W. Sockman

CHAPTER ONE

"There's a new chieftain of the Aerasceatle clutch."

Basques Grouper lifted one brow as he focused on his coven master, Krispin Stearling.

The coven's second, Ridger Carruthers asked what Basques was thinking. "That's unusual, isn't it? I didn't think Chieftain Grecian was even close to stepping down. Hostile takeover?"

Krispin dipped his black-haired head in the slightest of nods. "Yes. One of the enforcers challenged and wrestled control from the chieftain." His blue eyes narrowed as he absently stroked his goatee. "Rumors are there was even a gargoyle elder in attendance."

"An elder?" Basques lifted his tumbler of whiskey and swirled the contents as he thought about that. "The gargoyle race only has a few of them, don't they?"

Krispin nodded once more. "Twelve, if memory serves."

"And the elder backed the takeover?" Ridger commented before taking a sip of his own drink. "Huh."

Basques thought the same thing. The gargoyle race had always been known as fairly passive. While they defended their interests with blood-thirsty intensity, they didn't go out of their way to attack others. If this gargoyle was willing to roust his own chieftain, did that mean he was different?

Their coven was only a couple hundred miles away, situated in the city of Green Springs. They'd always had an unspoken agreement with Chieftain Grecian to leave each other alone. An ambitious gargoyle could spell trouble for them.

1

"I think we need to meet this new chieftain" — Master Krispin glanced down and checked his notes — "Chieftain Kinsey and see what his intentions are." He glanced around the room, peering at not only Ridger and Basques but the coven's second enforcer, Tabatha, who was also sitting in on the meeting. "We need a gift suitable for a new chieftain. Ideas?"

"Without knowing much about him, we should probably do something classic," Basques offered before taking a sip of his whiskey. "Something that can't be misconstrued as offensive."

"A cask of mead?" Ridger tossed out the idea.

"Does he have a beloved?" Tabatha asked even as she nodded, obviously liking Ridger's idea.

Either that or she was trying to get in the man's bed again. Basques had heard she had managed to snag Ridger's attention for one evening, but since they weren't beloveds, he had been clear he wasn't interested in a repeat. Tabatha was still trying to change his mind.

Basques intended to pull Ridger aside and warn him of the rumor he'd just overheard that Tabatha was hoping to have a baby with him. Something about strong genetics, and how it would set the kid up for greatness. While Tabatha was ambitious, she'd hit the ceiling of where she could rise at the Maven coven, so Basques's sources said she wanted to have a powerful child so she could eventually start her own coven.

She even had a few vampires convinced to go with her.

Hmm . . . maybe I should let Master Krispin know, too.

"Yes, Chieftain Kinsey is mated." Krispin's response returned Basques's attention to the here and now. "A young human male named Jimmy."

Tabatha's brows furrowed. "A human male?" She snickered before adding, "How will he produce an heir, then? That seems foolish on Fate's part. Maybe he's not a true mate but someone he's infatuated with?"

Basques fought his desire to roll his eyes as he stated, "You forget, Tabatha." When she pinned a narrow-eyed gaze at him, he barely resisted the urge to bare his fangs or smack the disrespectful look off her face. "Gargoyles can reproduce with their male partners."

"Oh my god!" Tabatha cried, curling her lip and wrinkling her nose as if she'd just smelled something disgusting. "That's horrible!"

Master Krispin's eyes narrowed as he held up his hand, obviously calling for her silence.

Tabatha made the mistake of not heeding his warning. "That's so unnatural," she griped, shaking her head. "How come I hadn't heard that before? I always thought gargoyles were sort of monster-like, but now I know they're—"

"Enough," Master Krispin thundered, rising from his seat. Pointing toward the door, he ordered in a cold tone, "Go find Carmine. Now."

Rising to her feet, Tabatha nodded curtly. Then she headed out of the room.

When she slammed the door behind her, Second Ridger groaned. "Gods, I can't believe I tapped that." He rubbed his palm over his face as he shook his head.

Basques barked a laugh, unable to help himself. Even the master snorted a quiet chuckle. Heaving a sigh, Ridger scowled at them both.

"I was gonna warn you," Basques began, pointing toward the door with his tumbler. "She's trying to get you to knock her up. She wants a powerful child, so she can start her own coven."

Ridger's cheeks paled, and his eyes widened. He began shaking his head, then stopped in favor of gulping the rest of his whiskey. After that, he rose and crossed to the sideboard to refill his glass. Once he'd downed it like a shot, Ridger huffed a sigh.

"Please tell me you're making that shit up," Ridger muttered, refilling his tumbler again.

"I heard that rumor, too, old friend," Krispin claimed, rising from his own seat. He rounded his desk to stand next to Ridger, placing his hand on his shoulder, all pretense of rank dropped with only the three of them in the room. They'd started the coven together over one hundred fifty years before. "I've had Sorbin keeping a discreet eye on her for the last month," he admitted, referencing one of the coven's best trackers.

"Gods, Kris," Ridger replied, heaving a sigh. "I didn't mean to cause trouble by sleeping with her. I was—" He paused and shook his head.

Basques rose and joined them, grabbing the whiskey decanter from Ridger. "You were off your game after watching one of your favorite donors run across a panther shifter in town and end up being his mate." While Basques spoke, he refreshed his drink, then offered Krispin a drink, which he accepted. "You were drunk and probably not being too discerning about what body you wanted to get lost in."

Ridger winced as he took a sip of his drink. Then he nodded as he headed back to his chair. After flopping onto it, he heaved a huge sigh.

"At least you remembered a condom," Krispin teased, leaning his butt against his desk and resting one ankle over the other. He winked as Ridger scoffed, taking a drink of his whiskey. After swallowing, Krispin stated, "So, I like the idea of sending them a barrel of mead. One or two?"

Basques knew their friend was changing the subject in an effort to spare Ridger's feelings. No one wanted to be reminded of doing something stupid. Besides, there'd been no harm in Ridger's actions.

Settling on the arm of the huge cushioned chair he'd been seated in earlier, Basques placed his foot on the cushion. "I like the idea of two barrels, but would that be seen as too much?"

"I don't think so," Ridger countered. "The monetary worth of them would be a reminder of our wealth and power as well as an offer to keep the truce we have between our coven and their clutch."

Krispin nodded. "Sounds good." He tipped his glass in Ridger's direction before taking a sip. Then he told them, "I'll put in a request for you to visit. Go with Ridger, Basques. And take Carmine with you, too."

Basques frowned as he rested his drink on his knee. "You sure everything will be okay here with us taking the fourth enforcer, too?"

For some reason, the hairs on Basques's nape stood on end at the idea of leaving his master with only the third-ranking enforcer, Pierce, for back-up when Tabatha was clearly working to make waves.

Krispin grinned widely as he licked his fangs. At the same time, he lengthened his claws and allowed his blue eyes to haze to red. A low, dark chuckle rumbled from the master.

"Don't worry about me, my friend," Krispin growled softly, winking at him. "If she starts shit while you're away, it could be a fun workout." Then he allowed his eyes to return to normal and withdrew his claws. "Besides, we still have a half dozen trackers at the coven, and I know they're *all* loyal to me."

Ridger laughed softly as he pointed at Basques. "He's got ya there." Then he furrowed his brows upon seeing the way Basques rubbed the back of his neck. "You got a feeling?"

Basques nodded, discomfort filling him. "Yeah." His friends might razz him a little about always trusting his gut, but over the decades, they'd come to trust him when he felt unsettled about something. "If it's not about the inner problems of our coven, then maybe it's about this upcoming meeting?"

Krispin exchanged a look with Ridger, then met his gaze and nodded. "Could be. Don't worry. I won't roust Tabatha from her position until you all get back, so rest easy on that front," he offered, obviously attempting to reassure him. "As for the meeting with the gargoyles, why don't you take one of the trackers in training just for an extra set of eyes, ears, and claws?"

Nodding, Ridger stated, "How about Kraymer?"

"Sounds good." Krispin grabbed his phone from the desk and started dialing. "I'll get this set up, so we can set ourselves at ease."

"Or get ready for a fight," Ridger muttered.

Basques silently agreed as he sipped his whiskey and listened to his coven master request a meeting to offer a gift.

Three days later, Basques drove a coven SUV deep into the woods. Second Ridger sat in the passenger seat, staring out the windshield. Enforcer Carmine and Tracker Kraymer sat in the middle captains chairs.

As they turned to head down a long, winding driveway, Kraymer leaned forward and asked, "Have you guys ever met a gargoyle before?"

Basques glanced in his rearview mirror at the excited expression on the young tracker's face. At barely thirty-eight, the vampire was still considered wet behind the ears, regardless of his extraordinary aptitude for tracking. Times like these reminded Basques of that fact.

"Yeah," Ridger answered. "We visited this clutch almost fifty years ago and met with Chieftain Grecian." Smirking, he added, "He was sort of a dick."

"Hopefully Chieftain Kinsey will be an improvement,"

Basques commented. Then he admitted, "But if he was brut-ish enough to fight through the inner circle and still beat Grecian, well . . . I'm not holding out much hope."

"Remember to be on your best behavior," Ridger warned. "We would prefer to keep the peace."

"Why would they want a fight, anyway?" Kraymer asked, his confusion clear in his tone. "What use would living near a city be to gargoyles in hiding?"

"Maybe to help them find mates easier?" Carmine guessed before shrugging his wide shoulders. "Doesn't matter. That's our home, and they can't have it." He grinned, showing off his fangs. "But I'll be good."

Ridger snorted. "Glad to hear it."

"Especially since we're here," Basques commented with a chuckle, parking the vehicle to the left of the large lodge-style home's big, four-car garage. "You two pull the mead barrels out of the back while we knock."

"Yes, sir," both men replied almost in unison.

As soon as Basques slipped from the vehicle, the hairs on his nape once again stood on end. He ignored the desire to rub them, unwilling to betray his unease. As paranormals, the gargoyles would be able to scent it easily enough as it was.

"Looks like the welcoming party," Ridger murmured as soon as Basques joined him beside the passenger door.

Basques followed his second's gaze to the front door, which stood open. Three gargoyles were standing on the deck. All three stood well over six feet tall, probably pushing six-foot-six and up. As was traditional for a gargoyle, they all wore a loincloth around their hips, which showcased their thickly muscled torsos and limbs.

The biggest of the lot at around six-foot-ten, a dark-green gargoyle, spoke as Basques and Ridger approached.

"Welcome to the Aerasceatle clutch," he greeted, holding out his black-clawed hand. "I'm Second Destrawn."

"Second Ridger," the vampire greeted, taking the male's hand. "And this is Head Enforcer Basques. Thank you for allowing us in your people's territory today."

Destrawn offered a wide, toothy smile. "You come bearing aged mead, so of course, we'd say yes." He took a step backward as he chuckled. "That and we know your coven was on cordial terms with this clutch's prior chieftain. It's only natural that you'd want to meet the new one." Beckoning, Destrawn added, "Come on. I'll introduce you to Chieftain Kinsey."

Basques flanked Ridger, falling into step at his left shoulder. He noticed that Carmine and Kraymer handed off the mead barrels to the other pair of gargoyles who'd been waiting on the porch. Then the vampire pair flanked Basques and Ridger.

Destrawn led the way down the hall and through a door on the right, not caring in the least when the pair with the mead went another direction. Basques figured the massive, six-foot-ten gargoyle was either confident in his skills or figured they weren't a threat. When they entered the room, Basques decided it was a little bit of both.

Three others waited.

A big, broad gargoyle with yellowish-orange skin stood on the far side of the large great room near the fireplace. He was the shortest at around six-foot-six and had his arm around a small, slender human. A powder-gray gargoyle stood near a sofa, and he split the difference at six-foot-eight.

Gods, I forgot how big these fuckers can be.

As Basques had suspected, the male holding the human introduced himself as Chieftain Kinsey. The human was his mate, Jimmy. Basques learned that the gray male was Enforcer Sethnos.

They had just finished introductions and pleasantries when a soft knock sounded on the door. Second Destrawn crossed to the door and opened it, revealing a gargoyle smaller than Basques had ever seen before. He was pushing a trolley which held an array of drinks and finger foods.

The pale-blue-hided gargoyle only stood five-foot-ten, and his long white hair hung almost to his waist, even in the half dozen braids it was kept in. Not only that, but the male didn't appear to have any wings, although Basques did spot some extra folds of skin along his underarms and sides.

Huh. Odd.

Just as Basques turned his attention back to Chieftain Kinsey, who was offering them refreshments, a rich, earthy scent tickled his senses. Inhaling deeply, Basques almost groaned. The mouth-watering fragrance seemed to combine with blood-rich iron in a way that slammed him with lust.

For the first time in centuries, Basques's control slipped. His eyes hazed as he riveted his gaze back on the little gargoyle. Groaning, he mapped the heated lines flowing through the small male.

Realization hit.

Holy shit! I think this male is my beloved.

In hindsight, Basques realized he should have said *that* out loud, but instead, he blurted, "Gods, I want your blood in the worst way."

CHAPTER TWO

Dloben's tension was already through the roof. He could hardly smell anything *except* his nerves—just the rich scent of coffee from the carafe on the cart he pushed. He wasn't supposed to have been the guy serving the refreshments, but his fellow gargoyle, Praerna, had begged him to take his shift. Evidently, the man had wanted to meet up with a group of friends online to play some kind of video game together.

He'd said this was the only time all four of the other guys could get together . . . otherwise, it would be a week before they could complete whatever mission they were trying to do.

So on top of working until sunup the previous evening in the garden, Dloben had to wake and head to the kitchen first thing. Then he would have to return to the garden after the kitchen shift. Dloben loved his new job working in the garden, helping to grow the food instead of cooking it.

Not only was it quiet work, but it was also solitary, too.

Dloben preferred solitary. His life before Kinsey had become chieftain had been damn near hell. His back bore the scars, too.

And it wasn't easy to scar a gargoyle.

Before softly knocking on the closed door of the great room, Dloben had taken several long, calming breaths. He knew Enforcer Kinsey—*crap, Chieftain Kinsey*—wasn't a sadistic, controlling alpha personality like Grecian was. Still, walking into a room where he knew not only were the gargoyle inner circle clustered, but there would be powerful vampires, scared the shit out of him.

If Dloben wore boots, he would have been shaking in them.

Second Destrawn had welcomed him with a soft greeting. The huge green male was a new addition to the clutch, and while strict in adhering to hierarchy rules and schedules, he was always kind. Well, unless someone fucked up — like, really, *really* fucked up — then Destrawn carried out his discipline duties with the same firmness as anything else.

Of course, so far, none of the punishments prescribed had been of the physical variety.

Dloben loved the change, but he didn't trust it, yet. It was too soon, so he always stayed on his toes. When he wasn't required to work, he kept to himself.

So when a huge vampire dressed all in black pinned him with a heated gaze, Dloben would have thought him sexy if it hadn't been for the red irises of his eyes. Hearing the vampire demand his blood caused his nerves to erupt into all-out panic. Squeaking in alarm, Dloben turned and fled.

Racing through the huge lodge, Dloben reached his room. He slammed the door behind him, then locked it for good measure. Finally, he crawled into the closet and shut the door.

Dloben's frame shook where he curled up on the floor. Tucking his knees to his chest with his back against the wall, he stared through the crack he'd left. He struggled to get his breathing to slow so he could hear if anyone came in.

As soon as his frantic thoughts began to unscramble, Dloben hid his face in his knees. Shame and embarrassment flooded him. He groaned roughly as he shook his head, rolling his forehead over his bony flesh.

"Gods, I'm hiding in a closet like a scared hatchling." His grumbled words didn't convince him to get up, however. Lifting his head, he rested it against the wall behind him. "And it's stupid, because any paranormal could track me here, breaking locks along the way."

Except, Dloben knew the response to fear wasn't always a rational thing.

A soft knocking on his door caught Dloben's attention. He froze, a fresh wave of trembles working through him. The voice he heard through the door reassured him somewhat.

"Dloben? Can you answer the door for me, please?" Chieftain Kinsey called, his tone gentle. "It's just me out here."

After taking another couple of slow, deep breaths, Dloben forced himself to his feet. He crept out of the closet and crossed his small room. Upon reaching the door, he inhaled deeply, scenting who was on the other side of the door.

While Dloben figured it was rude to second guess his chieftain, it was too ingrained in him. Chieftain Grecian would have pulled such a trick. On the other hand, Grecian wouldn't have knocked.

Dloben turned the knob and tugged the door open just a little. Then he took a step backward. Crossing his arms over his chest, he hugged himself as he bowed his head before his chieftain.

"I'm sorry," Dloben immediately murmured.

"You have nothing to apologize for," Chieftain Kinsey told him. He rested his hand on Dloben's shoulder as he used his other to close the door, enclosing them in the room.

"But I didn't serve the refreshments," Dloben replied, confusion filling him. He rubbed at his arms uneasily as he forced himself to peer at his chieftain's face through his lashes. "And I didn't ask permission to leave."

"I already know the reason you left." Chieftain Kinsey's lips curved into a small smile that looked a little on the worried side. "Can we sit? There's been a misunderstanding."

Dloben nodded even as he crossed to the bed. Sitting upon it, he watched his chieftain grab his desk chair. Kinsey spun it around and straddled it backward, resting his arms on the back.

Once settled, Kinsey met his gaze. "Did you know that a vampire can't confirm their beloved unless they taste their blood?"

Shaking his head, Dloben admitted his ignorance. "Really? Why would Fate do that?"

And what did it have to do with anything?

"Probably because a vampire drinks blood to survive. That person would taste them anyway." The chieftain shrugged. "But even before they confirm that someone is their beloved, they're drawn to that someone." He smiled as he added, "Kinda like how Basques wanted your blood."

"Is that his name?" Dloben whispered, shivering at the reminder.

"It is," Kinsey confirmed. "He's the head enforcer for the nearby Maven coven that's visiting."

The vampire was big, broad, and hot, but he was scary, too. When his eyes had turned red, Dloben had acted on instinct— running for his life. His fear had overridden every thought.

"Why does he want to hurt me?" Dloben rubbed at his knees before whispering, "W-Will you protect me? Did you, did you send them away?"

Kinsey shook his head, causing a spike of trepidation to stab through Dloben. Evidently, his chieftain had smelled the shift in his scent, for he lifted his hand in placation. "You just jumped to another conclusion, didn't you?"

Dloben began to shake his head, but the way Kinsey arched one brow ridge made him pause. Taking a few seconds, he thought about his chieftain's question. He did have a habit of doing that, but ever since his parents had been killed in a car accident two decades before, he'd had to interpret the intent of others to stay alive. Otherwise, Dloben would run amock of the wrong gargoyle. He'd become damn good at extrapolating the truth from just a few words and another person's scent.

Most of the old inner circle had enjoyed taunting the

smaller gargoyles.

Except, that had all changed when Kinsey took over.

While Dloben still stayed clear of a couple of larger gargoyles, most of the assholes had been weeded out and sent away. The elder that had overseen Kinsey and Grecian's fight had taken them. Dloben didn't know where they'd gone and didn't care.

"So, you *will* protect me?" Dloben hazarded softly.

"I will always protect you, Dloben," Chieftain Kinsey told him, giving him a gentle smile. "You're part of my clutch. And as your chieftain, your safety, security, and happiness is my responsibility." Kinsey grimaced as he shook his head. "Grecian lost sight of that somewhere along the way. I'm sorry for that."

"It wasn't your fault."

Kinsey smiled, nodding. "Right. And I shook my head because I didn't send them away."

Dloben frowned. "Because we need an alliance with them or something?"

"While I do want to be on friendly terms with the nearby coven, that's not the only reason." Kinsey narrowed his eyes as he added, "I'd hoped me explaining how vampires needed to taste their beloved's blood to confirm their bond, then recalling Basques's words, you'd make the correlation."

Frowning, Dloben just stared.

Huh?

Chuckling softly, Kinsey shook his head. "Basques definitely should have handled the situation differently, but the reason he said he wanted your blood was to taste it, not to hurt you." When Dloben continued to stare at his chieftain with what he knew was a confused expression, Kinsey reached out and touched his hand. "Basques thinks you're his beloved."

"What?" Dloben squeaked, jerking away from Kinsey's touch. He crab-walked backward on the bed until he was pressed against the headboard. As Kinsey rose and slowly strode toward him, Dloben could only stare.

"Calm down, Dloben," Kinsey urged as he reached for him. Sitting on the side of the bed, he gripped Dloben's leg in a gentle hold, but Dloben still flinched. "Tell me why finding your mate causes you such alarm. It's a blessing."

Dloben absently nodded, trying to explain what he was feeling. Then it hit him. "How come I didn't scent him as my mate?" Frowning, he met his chieftain's gaze. "Shouldn't I know, too?"

Kinsey hummed, obviously thinking. "You should, sure." Then he pinned Dloben with a serious look. "*If* you had scented him. Could you smell anyone in the room over the acrid aroma of your nerves?"

Grimacing, Dloben heaved a sigh. "No," he admitted.

"So are you willing to meet with Basques?"

Dloben knew he should say *yes*. Hell, any other gargoyle would probably jump at the chance. Unfortunately, Dloben wasn't any other gargoyle.

"What if he wants to take me away from here?" Dloben was finally beginning to feel comfortable at their large several-story, lodge-style home. "He's an enforcer, so what if he's mean?"

The vampire had looked . . . well, not mean *exactly* — fierce, rather. He'd been big and broad, easily determined even though he'd been sitting down. With the black leather pants he wore and the tight, black t-shirt, his muscles had been on clear display.

"Dloben." Kinsey said his name in a chiding manner. "If he *is* your mate, then he wouldn't be mean to you." He squeezed Dloben's thigh gently. "But you're right. You may end up having to live at the coven, since he's in their inner circle. As your mate, though, he'd want you happy."

Heaving a sigh, Dloben muttered, "Another change."

"Well, not until you meet him first." Kinsey rose to his feet and faced him squarely. "Should I tell him you need more time to calm down? Or do you want to meet him now?"

"Will you stay in the room?" Dloben figured the vampire might think him a wuss, but he couldn't help it.

Kinsey nodded. "Absolutely. I'll stay until you tell me to go."

"Okay." Sliding to the edge of the bed, Dloben swung his feet to the floor. "Let's go."

Chuckling, Kinsey led the way. "You don't have to make it sound like you're going to your death."

Dloben nibbled his lower lip, but he decided not to reply. His life had seen one too many changes over the last fifty years. At least the last one—Kinsey taking over the clutch—had been a good one.

Please, gods, let this change be a good one, too.

Holding onto that thought and prayer, Dloben followed Kinsey out of his room. He didn't take him back to the front lounge. Instead, they headed toward the rear of the home.

"I recall how much you enjoy the gardens, so I had Destrawn take Basques there." Kinsey winked at him. "More romantic, too, right?"

Dloben shrugged, unwilling to comment.

Chieftain Kinsey squeezed his shoulder before releasing him and grabbing the door. "Try to relax a little, okay?" he murmured before leading the way outside.

Crossing the back patio—the place lit up with tiki torches—Dloben paused at the edge. He took in the man's short, light-brown hair and goatee. The guy appeared to be lounging on a bench near a section of tulip beds. The tension in his shoulders, however, screamed his unease.

Beside him sat another man, a blond man with light-brown eyes. The man had his hand on Basques's shoulder as if keeping him in place. He was also murmuring something to him, while Basques scowled at the ground.

"That's the coven's second, Ridger Carruthers," Chieftain Kinsey murmured.

Dloben nodded.

Makes sense the second would be in on the meeting, considering how the last one had gone.

The sound of Kinsey speaking must have drawn their attention. Both men snapped their focus to them. Dloben watched as Basques swept his gaze up and down his frame, but his expression remained blank, not giving away his thoughts.

Basques made a move to stand, but Ridger's hand on his shoulder stopped him. Casting a frown the second's way, the darker vampire growled.

"Relax, remember?" Ridger responded, not at all fazed by Basques's ire.

The angry look affected Dloben, however. He wrapped his arms around himself and shifted uneasily. Still too far away to scent the vampire, he struggled with getting his feet to move.

"Take your time, Dloben," Kinsey encouraged him, crossing to another bench near where the vampires sat. In a louder voice, he stated, "As I told you earlier, Basques, this is Dloben, and he has reason to be skittish."

"But you won't tell me what reason," Basques responded slowly, his gaze cutting from the chieftain to Dloben and back again.

Upon hearing Basques's deep voice again, a shiver went down Dloben's spine. Feeling a little calmer, however, he realized it wasn't from fear. He wasn't panicking, either.

"It's not my story to tell, Basques," Chieftain Kinsey countered, shaking his head.

Dloben once again found himself the recipient of Basques's deep blue-eyed stare. When he licked his lips and swallowed, he found the way the vampire stared at his mouth created a trickle of something warm in his belly.

That's good, right?
Gathering his courage, Dloben slowly started forward.

CHAPTER THREE

Basques practically vibrated in his seat. Only Ridger's hand on his shoulder kept him still. Good thing, too, since he could see how nervous the small gargoyle still was.

Hadn't the chieftain explained?

When Dloben's tongue slipped out and wet his lips, Basques found his gaze riveted to the movement. He wanted to follow the move with his own tongue. Then he would —

"Relax," Ridger urged, his tone dry. "Jumping the gargoyle isn't going to win you any points."

Basques sucked in a harsh breath, nodding. He let it out on a deep sigh. After the gargoyle had run from the room, Basques had been read the riot act until he'd admitted he thought the small, blue gargoyle was his beloved. Then everyone in the room had warned him to be patient and go slow.

Gods, can I do that? I'm not known for my patience.

For his beloved, Basques would try.

Knowing he really needed to get his mind off his hard dick, he thought of something else — his need to apologize.

As one of the inner circle, Basques didn't have to do it often, and he sucked at it. Again, for his beloved, he could do it. At least finding the words caused his erection to deflate, a little, anyway.

"I wish to apologize for my outburst earlier," Basques began slowly. He watched as Dloben slowly moved closer. The gargoyle's pale-green-eyed gaze darted this way and that, but to Basques's pleasure, it always returned to him. Remembering the chieftain's warning and seeing Dloben's skittishness himself, Basques lowered his voice to a gentle tone and added, "I'm over two hundred years old and had never scented anything like the amazing aroma of your blood."

Dloben reached the nearby bench where Chieftain Kinsey sat and settled gingerly on the edge of it. He looked prepared to flee at the slightest provocation. His pale-blue hide had a faint glow to his cheeks, and he peered at Basques from beneath his thick lashes.

When Dloben flicked out his tongue, licking his lips again, Basques suddenly remembered a bit of trivia he'd heard years before. Gargoyles had hundreds of scent receptors on their tongue. Dloben was smelling him.

Flicking his focus to Dloben's groin, Basques just managed to suppress his grin. His little gargoyle wasn't unaffected by him after all. There was a very lovely front-bump growing beneath the brown bit of cloth.

To Basques's surprise, a surge of possessive jealousy shot through him when he realized everyone else would be able to see the pretty bulge, too.

Gods, don't be an asshole.

With that thought in mind, Basques tried again. "The smell of your blood rocked my world, Dloben," he rumbled softly, leaning forward and resting his forearms on his thighs just to be a tiny bit closer to the obviously scared gargoyle. "My words were careless, but all I meant was that I wished to try a drop to confirm my suspicion that you're my beloved." Even though he was trying to be patient, Basques had to ask, "I understand a gargoyle can scent their mate straight away. Why did you run if we're mates?"

A niggle of unease wormed its way into Basques's mind.

Does my beloved not want me?

Gods, that would suck.

"It's not that simple," Dloben finally whispered.

The pleasant sound of his tenor voice felt like a shot straight to Basques's balls. His prick twitched in his leather pants, and a dollop of pre-cum oozed from him. He cleared his throat as he straightened, shifting in his seat, trying to get more room behind the crotch of his pants.

Dloben's beautiful blue hide flushed a bit darker as his gaze flicked to Basques's groin, then back up again.

"Then please tell me, beautiful," Basques murmured, trying to get them on track when all he wanted was to lunge forward, grab his beloved and toss him over his shoulder, then spirit him away from some horizontal fun. "Tell me why you'd run from your mate."

"I didn't know you were my mate," Dloben blurted out, rubbing his white-clawed hands over his slender thighs. "I didn't scent you."

That stopped Basques in his tracks.

"What?" *How is that possible?* "Why?" Basques cocked his head. "Are you injured in some way?"

"Yes." Then Dloben's slender eyebrow ridges furrowed. "No." He shook his head. "Not like that."

"I'm confused," Basques admitted. He glanced toward Ridger, who shrugged.

Dloben peered Chieftain Kinsey's way. The big gargoyle gave Dloben an encouraging smile as he stated, "Take your time. Nothing you say here will land you in any trouble." Chieftain Kinsey leveled a serious look at him and the second. "Right?"

Basques immediately nodded, ready to agree to just about anything to get things moving forward again.

"Of course," Second Ridger assured.

"F-First—" Dloben slowly rose from his seat. "Might as well know for sure."

Even as Dloben mumbled the words, he took a slow step forward. Lifting both hands, he dug the claw of his forefinger into the palm of his left hand. The deep, rich-colored fluid welled up from between his split flesh.

The heady scent hit Basques's senses, and a deep groan ripped from his throat. His mouth watered. Swallowing hard, Basques licked his lips as he glanced between the blood pooling in Dloben's palm and his most-likely beloved's face.

Seeing Dloben extend his bloodied, cupped hand, Basques reached for it, finding that his own hand was trembling.

Fuck! You're over two hundred years old. Pull yourself together!

"Glad I'm not the only one nervous," Dloben whispered.

Just that fast, Basques's unease vanished. He grinned up at Dloben as he gently cradled the gargoyle's blue wrist. "Not every day you meet someone who calls to your nature, beautiful." Then he stuck out his tongue and gently slid it along Dloben's palm.

The first thing that hit him was the salty tang of Dloben's flesh. After that, his appendage wiped through the well of blood. A burst of exquisite flavor flared across his tongue.

The sweetest flavor erupted, causing his senses to flare to life.

Moaning, Basques quickly lapped for more. On the third lick, he moaned for a different reason. Due to the healing properties of his saliva, coupled with a gargoyle's naturally swift recuperative ability, the wound was nearly closed.

Basques was so damn tempted to pull Dloben's wrist to his lips and sink in his fangs. He would do damn near anything to enjoy more of his beloved's delicious, life-giving fluid.

Only the pain to his shoulder stayed the action, and when he released Dloben's wrist, he forced a warm look as he licked his lips of every trace of his gargoyle's fluid.

"No mistake," Basques said on a moan. "You're mine." He turned his attention to Ridger and muttered, "Thanks."

Only then did Ridger ease his grip.

Holy fucking hell. A few drops of Dloben's blood and I'm about ready to lose myself.

Basques hadn't had that happen since he was just coming out of puberty and figuring out how to control his impulses.

Wow!

He wasn't certain if he liked that or not.

Dismissing the disturbing thought, Basques watched Dloben return to the bench where Chieftain Kinsey sat. He almost resumed his own seat but paused. Bobbing his head in a nod, as if confirming something to himself, Dloben met his gaze.

"I'm not beautiful. I was abused by the prior inner circle." Dloben crossed his arms over his chest, then turned and showed his back. "That's why I have trouble with dominant men."

Basques just held in his gasp upon spotting the slender lines of scarring criss-crossing Dloben's back. His sweet blue beloved had been brutalized. He clenched his hands, fighting his desire to grab his beloved and take him away from the clutch and its horrible members.

He barely resisted, knowing that would just freak out his skittish gargoyle.

And these members aren't the ones who harmed him. Or are they?

When Basques found his voice, he couldn't stop the growl in his tone. "Thank you for removing that bastard from leadership," he snarled gruffly. "Are there any left here that harass you, Dloben?"

Seeing Dloben turn to face him, Basques did his best to clear the anger from his features. He didn't want his little beloved to think it was geared at him. Instead, he managed to offer the man he soon hoped to make his lover an encouraging smile.

"Please talk to me," Basques urged. Lifting his hand, he waved at Dloben's body while adding, "And scars show your strength, beautiful. Nothing more." Basques rubbed at his side absently. "I have a few of my own."

Dloben cocked his head, then nodded. "There's still a few jerks around that I avoid," he admitted, slowly resettling back on the bench next to his chieftain. "Don't you have jerks in your coven?"

Basques nodded once. "I suppose so."

"Who's been hassling you?" Chieftain Kinsey asked, annoyance filling his tone. "Is it just you or are there others, too?"

Sighing deeply, Dloben only shrugged.

Not a talker. Good to know. Of course, that meant communication could be tough. Good thing I'm a vampire, and we'll end up with a mental link.

While Basques knew that taking a peek into his gargoyle's mind could be considered intrusive, he would do anything and use any advantage to help his frightened beloved.

It was Chieftain Kinsey's turn to sigh. "Dloben." He rested his clawed hand on Dloben's shoulder. "I can't fix a problem if I don't know about it."

"I don't want to get anyone into trouble," Dloben replied.

"Oh, honey," Basques crooned, leaning forward as he swept his gaze over his beloved's hunched form. "If someone is hassling you, then they need to be stopped."

Dloben nibbled his bottom lip once more, and Basques's mouth watered with his desire to do the same. Finally, the gargoyle dipped his head in a nod. "Chasis and his buddy Ducine will push us around if they run across me or one of the smaller gargoyles alone."

Chieftain Kinsey growled under his breath as he nodded. "Okay. I'll put a watch on them."

Basques scowled at the big male. "You can smell that he's telling the truth," he pointed out indignantly.

"No, it's okay," Dloben cut in, lifting his hand in a placating manner. He even offered a small smile. "He needs to catch them in the act, or they'll just say they understand and keep on doing the behavior." Dloben's focus slid to the side. "Everyone was warned, so they could just try to play it off as goofing around."

While Basques didn't like it, he understood. "Okay, then,"

he commented slowly. "Can we talk about us, Dloben?"

"Us?" Dloben rubbed his palms over his thighs as he peered at him through his lashes. "What do you think we should say?"

"I told you that you're my beloved, and I've tasted your blood." Basques watched as Dloben's face took on a pinkish hue, which was an interesting shade against his blue hide. "Do you recognize me as your mate?"

Basques wasn't certain what he would do if his beloved denied him.

"Yes," Dloben whispered. "Now that I've scented you, I know you're my mate."

"Good." Basques smiled widely. "Can we share a meal and get to know each other, Dloben?" Glancing between the pair, he admitted, "I've never seen a gargoyle of your size before. Do you have the ability to fly, too?"

Dloben opened his mouth, then closed it again. "Ch-Chieftain Grecian considered us small gargoyles second-class citizens," he muttered, lowering his gaze to the ground. "A labor class, so he would never have any of us appear in a meeting, so—" Dloben shifted on his seat as he swallowed hard enough to cause his Adam's apple to bob. "Not surprising you wouldn't have met one like me before."

Chieftain Kinsey growled low in his throat. "He was a fucking asshole, and you know that's not true, right?"

The way Dloben shrugged one shoulder set Basques's teeth on edge. "Dloben, can Chieftain Kinsey and I switch seats?" He desperately wanted to comfort his clearly upset beloved.

Dloben glanced around the group, opening and closing his mouth like a fish.

Basques felt his heart hammering in his chest. He silently willed Dloben to accept. To his pleasure, Dloben slowly began nodding.

"Okay," Dloben whispered, clenching and unclenching his

fists. "A-And we could eat together. Talk about . . . stuff."

Considering that a win, Basques rose from his seat. Chieftain Kinsey did the same. While Basques settled on the big gargoyle's vacated seat, Chieftain Kinsey took a few steps toward the patio before rocking back on one foot and appearing to get comfortable standing.

"It seems I must ask permission for Enforcer Basques to be able to stay for a few days," Ridger stated, also rising. He flashed a smile at them, then focused on the chieftain. "I'm sure you agree it will take time to mesh lives, even paranormals who know about the bond and hope it to happen to them one day."

Chieftain Kinsey nodded, resting his clawed hands on his hips. "Understandable." He turned his attention on Basques. "You can stay for the foreseeable future while you and Dloben get to know each other."

"Thank you, Chieftain," Basques said with a dip of his head in deference. Turning his attention to Dloben, he took a chance and slid his arm around his waist, resting his palm along his lower back, enjoying the unfamiliar sensation of his swarthy hide. "Do you wish to head to your dining hall for our meal? Or can we order something and take it to a more private place?"

For just an instant, Dloben leaned into his touch. Then he straightened on a gasp. "Oh, I'm supposed to be working right now."

Kinsey lifted his hand, palm out in placation. "I already have someone else stepping in."

"Oh . . . thank you." Dloben relaxed again as he nodded. "Okay. Um." He met Basques's gaze through his lashes. "Can we start in the dining hall and go from there, please?"

"Of course." Basques was quickly coming to realize that Dloben struggled with confidence and meeting someone else's gaze was tough for him. He hoped he could help his beloved with that, but he knew it would take time. Rubbing his hand up and down Dloben's spine in a light, soothing caress, Basques suggested, "Maybe after that, you can show me the favorite parts of your home."

"O-Okay."

With a gentle urge, Basques rose with Dloben beside him. He kept his arm around him as he headed toward the back of the house. Relishing the way his little gargoyle felt against his side, Basques almost missed Chieftain Kinsey and Ridger's next exchange.

"I'll stay out here and contact Master Krispin," Ridger told the chieftain. "Then return to the front room with the others. We can conclude our business whenever you're ready."

"Sounds good," Kinsey said with a nod. "Congratulations, Dloben."

"Thank you, Chieftain," Dloben responded softly.

"And don't forget to explain how gargoyle matings are slightly different than vampires," Chieftain added.

Pausing, Basques squeezed Dloben's hip to still him and keep him at his side. "What do you mean?" he asked, focusing on the bigger male.

Chieftain Kinsey lifted one brow ridge as he smirked at him. "Thought that would get your attention." His expression cleared, turning serious. "Seeing as you appear to be a pretty dominant fellow, I didn't know if Dloben would feel comfortable bringing it up for a while."

Basques opened his mouth, then snapped it shut again. Demanding that the chieftain just spit it out probably wasn't a smart move.

"In order for a gargoyle to go through molt and gain their human form, the bond must go both ways. Dloben must claim you, too."

It took Basques a few seconds before the chieftain's meaning sank in. His torso tensed as his chute clenched. He swallowed hard, forcing moisture into his suddenly too-dry throat.

"So, Dloben needs to top me," Basques muttered. As soon as he said the words, he understood why Dloben would have trouble telling him that.

Chieftain Kinsey lifted a hand in a so-so motion. "Well, there is the rare case of a gargoyle going through molt if his mate sucks him off enough, but I hear it's damn near agony, and going through molt is painful enough as it is."

Basques peered down at Dloben, but his sweet little gargoyle wouldn't meet his gaze.

Right. Don't want to cause my beloved more pain.

One way or another, Basques would figure out how to accept his gargoyle's cock up his ass.

Meeting the chieftain's gaze, Basques nodded. "Thank you for telling me."

For Dloben, I can do this . . . I hope.

CHAPTER FOUR

Dloben felt absolutely mortified. He couldn't believe his chieftain had just blurted it out like that. While it would have taken him a while, he really would have gotten around to sharing that . . . eventually.

And now it's just . . . out there.

Having noticed the way Basques had tensed beside him, Dloben knew the vampire didn't like the idea.

"We don't have to anytime soon," Dloben quickly reassured, clutching at his black t-shirt to get his attention. "I don't need to go through molt right away."

Basques squeezed his waist while giving him a slight smile. "I will never lie to you, sweet gargoyle," Basques vowed, bringing his other hand up and tracing down Dloben's jawline. "So I admit it does trouble me somewhat, but not enough to stop me from doing right by my beloved." Basques winked as he gave Dloben a hungry once-over. "Caring for *all* of each other's needs is part of the deal."

"Deal?" Dloben hadn't ever heard of it put that way before.

Waggling his brows at him, Basques rumbled, "Partnership? Relationship? Mating? Bonding?"

When he dipped his head, Dloben thought maybe he would kiss him, but instead, Basques nuzzled his goateed cheek against his own hairless one. It caused the skin of his neck to pebble in a warm, tingly way he'd never before experienced. Then when Basques spoke again, his warm breath wafting over his skin caused a shiver to work through him.

"Whatever you want to call it, my sweet gargoyle."

Basques gently suckled on the point of Dloben's ear, which caused his dick to jerk in his loincloth, and he nearly missed it when Basques stated, "We are in this together now. Your pleasure is my pleasure." His voice took on a low growling tone. "And I expect plenty of bliss and fun to be had between us."

"B-Bliss a-and fun sound good," Dloben managed to mutter, his brain barely able to formulate words.

"Maybe you should consider taking him to your room, Dloben," Chieftain Kinsey encouraged, his tone gentle. When Dloben forced his attention to his chieftain, the other gargoyle grinned widely as he added, "The pull to mate can get pretty intense, and while we only have a few, we wouldn't want any children stumbling across you if you get . . . distracted."

Dloben swallowed hard as Basques continued to tease his fingertips over his jawline and neck on one side. He used his mouth to gently map his ear and jaw on the other. Never in his life had Dloben felt such fantastic sensations, and he realized his chieftain was right.

Except, he didn't know if he was ready to jump straight into bonding.

Basques must have caught on to something of what Dloben was feeling, for he eased his ministrations. Straightening, the vampire smiled down at him. Gripping one of Dloben's braids, Basques gently massaged the lock between his fingertips.

"Sorry, Dloben," Basques murmured. A faint pinkish hue darkened the man's already medium complexion. "Your scent, the feel of your skin beneath my fingers . . ." He sighed, the sound one of happiness as he grinned at him. "Exquisite. Everything about you is exquisite."

Dloben didn't really think so, and part of him wondered if Basques would change his tune once they were alone. Girding up his courage—*there's only one way to find out*—he smiled tremulously at the vampire Fate had deemed his own. "I-I guess I could show you to my r-room." Upon seeing the surprise on Basques's face, Dloben quickly added, "I can order a meal, and w-we can t-talk."

"Are you sure?" Basques rubbed a hand over Dloben's shoulder. "No pressure." Then he chuckled roughly. "And I can keep my hands to myself."

"I don't want you to," Dloben blurted out, realizing it was true, too. Even feeling his cheeks heat, he added, "I like how you're touching me."

Basques groaned as he wrapped Dloben in a firm hug. "A meal and some alone time sounds amazing."

Dloben lifted his arms and tentatively returned his mate's hug. Since he wasn't used to touching others, it felt a little awkward but still nice. The way Basques rubbed up and down his back felt even nicer.

Easing away from Basques, Dloben reached down and took the big male's hand in a tentative grip. The vampire immediately smiled and threaded their fingers, squeezing gently. Dloben felt as if his heart skipped a beat, and something inside him eased.

"I'll have food delivered to you shortly, Dloben," Chieftain Kinsey assured.

Dloben nodded, then began leading the way through the large lodge-style home. He didn't really know what to say, so he pointed out the different spaces as they passed. The lodge was pretty big, all things considered, and there were two wings mirroring each other.

The west side of the home was definitely more opulent, since that had been where Chieftain Grecian, his inner circle, and the larger gargoyles had lived. The smaller gargoyles had rooms on the east side. Where the west side suites all had their own bathrooms, the east side rooms shared jack and jill bathrooms with someone.

The only thing that wasn't mirrored was the kitchen. Instead, a massive kitchen took up the space in the east wing, since until recently, it was run by the gargoyle's *second class*, as Grecian called it. That space in the west hall was the dining hall.

Chieftain Kinsey was in the process of inventorying rooms, moving people around, and renovating, but it was a lengthy process.

"I'm in here," Dloben stated as he opened his door. "It's not much."

Dloben watched anxiously as Basques closed the door behind them, then glanced around the space. It didn't even have a sofa, so Dloben didn't know why he was surprised when the vampire took his hand and led him to the bed. To his relief, all the man did was sit on the edge, tugging him down beside him.

"You're tense, handsome," Basques commented, rubbing his fingers lightly. "Want a massage?"

"A, uh, a massage?" Dloben cocked his head. "I don't think I've ever had one before."

Basques nodded, his expression thoughtful. "Then you don't know what you're missing." Tipping his head, he offered, "How about you lie on the bed on your stomach, and while I work your muscles, we can ask each other questions."

"W-Will it hurt?" Dloben asked, feeling wary at putting his back to a complete stranger—mate or not.

"Not if I'm doing it right." Basques fixed him with a serious look. "And if I do do something that hurts you, please tell me, and I won't do it again."

Dloben scented that Basques was telling him the truth, but how could he trust that. "What about biting me? Does it hurt when you drink my blood?"

Basques's eyes flashed red, and he sucked in a harsh breath. He moaned softly even as he shook his head. After a few blinks, his eyes returned to normal.

Taking advantage of Basques's distraction, Dloben pulled his hand away and slid further away from him.

When Basques fixed his gaze on him, he noticed the change, and a pained look flashed across his face. "Oh, Dloben, please don't fear me," he whispered roughly. Slowly reaching out his hand, he rested it on Dloben's thigh. "I would never harm you. Hearing you mention biting and me drinking your blood" — a shudder worked through the big male — "I'm so looking forward to it." Basques curved his lips into a warm smile. "There will be a pinch of pain, but only for an instant, then the most exquisite bliss will rush through you, and you'll come from the pleasure of it."

"Really?" Dloben had experienced plenty of pain, so a pinch didn't concern him. Seeing as he didn't know anything about vampires — or any other paranormals, for that matter — it just seemed a little farfetched. "How's that work?"

Basques rubbed his thigh lightly as he told him, "A vampire's saliva has an agent in it that removes the pain and causes pleasure." He leveled a hungry gaze on Dloben's face as he added, "Just as when you bite and claim me, I will find pleasure in it. I can hardly wait."

Dloben nodded, still a little disbelieving.

His brows furrowing, betraying his confusion, Basques asked, "Did no one explain the pleasures of bonding with your fated mate to you?"

Feeling suddenly shy, Dloben lifted one shoulder in a half-shrug. If he had to have this conversation already, he didn't want to see the disappointment on Basques's face when he did. Pulling away, Dloben slowly turned and crawled onto the bed.

After flopping on the bed, his arms to either side of his head, Dloben turned his head away from Basques. "I'm really young in terms of gargoyles," he admitted before heaving a sigh. "I'm sixty-seven, and my parents died when I was twenty-two. Car accident. I had a boyfriend once, but we didn't, uh . . . do much." Dloben closed his eyes as he whispered, "And I never talked to my parents about that. Like I said. They died when I was young, and we always thought we had more time. Then my parents were no longer there to protect me, and rule under Chieftain Grecian was unbearable, and finding someone I trusted to open up to wasn't—" Dloben cut off his rambling, hoping his mate wasn't too disappointed that he knew . . . next to nothing.

Dloben flinched with he felt Basques's hand on his back.

"Easy, sweetheart," Basques murmured, his tone husky. "You're okay."

Feeling the bed dip next to his hip, Dloben knew Basques was moving. At the same time, the vampire rubbed up and down his spine, lightly tracing the knobs there. Something soft brushed his shoulder, causing a tremble to work through him.

Dloben recognized Basques's soft goatee hair sliding along the back of his neck. "Thank you for telling me," he whispered, still nuzzling him. "I will be so damn gentle, Dloben. And have no fear, my beloved. We will love each other's bites." As if to reaffirm his statement, Basques nipped lightly at his earlobe, and it sent tingles down Dloben's neck. "We will crave them, crave each other."

Trembles working through him, Dloben scented the waves of arousal emanating from Basques. He didn't know what he'd said that the man appreciated so much. Turning his head, he peered over his shoulder at the vampire.

Basques smiled down at him. While his eyes held a reddish glow, emphasizing his desire for Dloben, his expression held a tenderness he hadn't seen in a long, long time. His heart ached when he realized that it hadn't been since his parents had died that someone had looked at him that way.

"Oh, sweet Dloben," Basques rumbled. "You really do not know your worth." Dipping his head, he pressed a light kiss to the corner of Dloben's mouth, then licked over his canine. "I will show you, my beloved."

Straightening, Basques rested on his knees. "Do you have any lotion?"

Dloben didn't understand the switch, but he nodded anyway. He pointed to his nightstand. "In there."

Basques leaned over and opened the drawer. He fumbled inside for a moment, then pulled out the requested item. After closing the drawer, he knee-walked backward a little as he popped open the cap.

"Now, I want you to relax and enjoy as we share a little about ourselves," Basques told him as he poured some lotion onto his palm before closing the tube. He rubbed his hands together. "I'm warming this a little, but it might still be a bit chilly. It should heat up soon."

Dloben nodded as he waited with anticipation that surprised him. "Okay." He didn't bother telling Basques that gargoyles had a much higher tolerance for hot and cold extremes due to their thicker hide.

All thought went out the window as Dloben felt the first firm caress of Basques's hands on his shoulders. The vampire kneaded and worked his muscles in a way that caused instant relaxation. He moaned softly, going limp beneath his ministrations.

"That is such a lovely response," Basques crooned. His voice, coupled with his smug scent, gave away his pride at what he was doing to Dloben. "Knew you'd like this."

Dloben let out a whimper in response, since right then, Basques began working down the knobs of his spine, and it felt glorious.

Basques chuckled, but it wasn't a cruel sound. He was just extremely pleased with himself. "So, you said you're young for a gargoyle at age sixty-seven. Guess that's young for just about any paranormal, but especially for your kind, right?" Before Dloben could untie his tongue to give an answer, Basques continued. "Is my information right that gargoyles can live upward of two thousand years?"

Fortunately, that question was easy. "Mmm-hmmm," Dloben hummed in response.

"Good." Basques leaned forward and pressed a kiss to Dloben's cheek, grinning at him. "That means we'll have a long, *long* time getting to know each other and enjoying each other's quirks." He winked, then straightened and continued with his massage.

When Basques slid his fingertips along Dloben's ribcage, he found the ridge along several that housed Dloben's bonespurs. He hummed, rubbing along them.

To Dloben's shock, waves of pleasure shot through him. He gasped and jerked beneath Basques's touch. Never had anyone touched him that way, and the intensity of the sensation shocked him.

"Dloben?" Basques asked, lifting his hands away. His concern filled his voice. "Are you okay? Did that hurt?"

Dloben shook his head even as he struggled to find his tongue. His cock ached against the fabric of his loincloth, and he was having a damn difficult time keeping himself from bucking his hips. He didn't know how to explain.

"Ah, erogenous zone for a gargoyle, then," Basques mused slowly, returning his hands to Dloben's back. His voice deepened, turning husky as he rubbed close to Dloben's bonespurs, but not directly on them again. "Do you have a name for this area, my beloved?"

Swallowing hard, Dloben rasped, "Th-Those are my bonespurs f-for my w-wingskins." He stretched his arms out a little, silently indicating the extra folds of skin that ran along the undersides of his arms and along his sides. "F-For flying."

"Ahhh," Basques purred, sliding his fingertips over the skin. "So you do fly. I'd love to see that."

Dloben groaned roughly, unable to help himself. The feel of Basques's fingers trailing over his wingskins was just as exquisite as him massaging his bone-spurs. He twitched and shifted, pressing into the vampire's touch, silently begging for more.

Basques growled low in his throat as he stilled his hands. "Easy, Dloben," he murmured, leaning close. "I didn't mean to start this, but I would so very much like to finish what we inadvertently began. Tell me this is okay."

Realizing his mate wanted permission, Dloben quickly nodded. "Yes!" he cried. "Gods, yes!"

Barking a cry of pleasure when Basques began exploring again, Dloben lost himself to the bliss of his mate touching him.

CHAPTER FIVE

Basques's arousal soared as he watched Dloben give himself over to the unexpected pleasure. His sweet gargoyle was so clearly touch-starved, and he relished being the one to fulfill his need. He couldn't wait to please Dloben every chance possible, showing him even more they could do together.

While it hadn't been Basques's intention to start something sexual between them when he'd offered the massage, there was no way he would deny Dloben once he'd realized his need.

And he's so beautiful when out of his mind with bliss.

Basques massaged along the ridges Dloben had told him were bone-spurs, causing his gargoyle to practically purr and arch into his touch. He found three on each side of his ribcage, and Dloben loved having them all touched. When Basques gently scraped his nails over his beloved's flaps of skin, he whined as he shuddered and trembled.

Then something odd happened.

The bone-spurs extended, stretching the skin.

Pausing an instant as he watched in fascination, Basques swept his focus over him in amazement.

So that's what he meant.

The whine of protest yanked Basques back to what he was supposed to be doing. He returned to his ministrations, sliding his hands over Dloben's skin and mapping his body. Keeping his hands above the waistline of his loincloth was difficult, since he was damn tempted to grab the gargoyle's lashing tail.

Unfortunately, since Basques didn't know how Dloben would take that, he resisted.

Without warning, Dloben froze beneath him, then began twitching as his hips bucked. Basques scented the heady fragrance of his gargoyle's cum perfuming the air, and his own aching dick gave a twitch. Upon hearing Dloben's clearly satisfied moan, Basques couldn't help it . . . his cock had been hard too long.

Basques let out a low groan of his own as he gritted his teeth while unloading into his leather pants. Mind-numbing endorphins filled him, sending him soaring. He swayed where he knelt on the bed, his senses reeling.

"Wow."

Dloben's slurred whisper jolted Basques back to the here and now. He chuckled roughly as he nodded. "Yeah. Totally."

When Dloben peered over his shoulder at him, already working his lower lip, Basques figured that probably wasn't what he should have said. *Right. Inexperienced. Needs reassurance.* The thoughts flitted through his mind, but since his brain was still mush, he simply grunted and flopped down next to his new and final lover.

"Um, I-I-I didn't mean—"

Hearing Dloben's stuttered words, coupled with the spike of his anxiety filling the room, overshadowing the sweet smell of their spent pleasure, Basques pulled his head out of his ass. "Easy, my beloved." He slid his arms around Dloben and pulled him close. "I loved what we did. Really. As unexpected as it was."

As Basques watched, Dloben's bone-spurs receded, easing the tautness of his wingskins. Basques trailed his fingertips over the smooth skin, unable to get enough of its softness. He also really liked the way Dloben shivered in his grip as he peered up at him.

"Don't be embarrassed. Please, beloved," Basques crooned, needing to get the scent of unease out of the air. "Watching you lose yourself in the bliss I gave you was the sexiest fucking thing I've ever seen."

Pulling his hand away from Dloben's smooth skin, Basques waved toward his own uncomfortable groin. It was never a good thing to lose your load in your pants, but somehow, leather made it worse. Still, Basques knew it was worth it.

"Oh!" Dloben stared up at him in shock. "Y-You—"

Basques smiled as he nodded, not forcing his sweet gargoyle to finish what he obviously thought was an embarrassing comment.

"I came in my pants like a teenager," Basques claimed, chuckling at himself while grinning. "You did that to me without even trying." Dipping his head, Basques pressed a kiss to Dloben's mouth. Then he relaxed again as he winked at the clearly shocked gargoyle. "Can't wait until you're actually trying. We'll be explosive."

"Is that good?"

Gods above, my beloved is so innocent. I look forward to changing that . . . in some ways.

Resting his hand on Dloben's jaw, Basques held his gargoyle's gaze with a serious look of his own as he nodded. "Do you kiss, Dloben?"

Basques eyed Dloben's square jaw and the way his canines poked out over his lips. With how his lover's mouth was constructed, he wasn't certain if that was something that was possible for the male. He sure hoped so, since he loved kissing, finding that it could be a wonderfully intimate experience.

"Yes," Dloben replied, sounding breathless.

Basques loved that he had that effect on his beloved. "May I kiss you?"

Dloben licked his lips, then nodded. "Yes, please."

More than on board with that, Basques lowered his head and gently pressed his lips to Dloben's. He licked around the gargoyle's canines gently before sliding his tongue between his slightly parted lips. Moving slowly, Basques mapped his lover's mouth, learning and exploring.

When Basques felt Dloben's slender appendage lap against his own, a pleasant tingle shot down his spine. His balls warmed, and his prick began to harden once more. Letting out a rough groan, he backed off the kiss and eased it to an end.

Grinning, Basques peered down at his gargoyle. "Wow, beautiful." Upon seeing Dloben's questioning look, he added, "Your kiss is amazing."

Basques loved the way Dloben's features darkened a bit in a blush even as he grinned shyly at him.

Feeling the itch in his groin intensify with his burgeoning erection, Basques groaned as he gave his gargoyle a wry smile. "Where's the closest bathroom? I'll get a cloth to clean us up."

Dloben's blush deepened. He nibbled his bottom lip as he pointed toward the door on the left. "Through there is a closet, then a bathroom. I share it with Praerna. He lives on the other side."

Nodding, Basques slipped from the bed. "Got it." Standing beside the bed, he traced the tips of his forefingers along Dloben's jawline as he smiled down at him. "Just relax here, my beloved, and rest."

Still nibbling on his lower lip, Dloben nodded.

Basques bent at the waist and pecked a kiss to his gargoyle's lips. Then he strode in the direction he'd been told. He opened the door and found a small closet. The shelves were mostly empty with what appeared to be a few folded loincloths stacked on one. The only other items there were towels, washcloths, and bathing supplies. There were several drawers on the left, and Basques found himself curious about what could be in them, if anything.

As Basques crossed to the door at the back of the space, he found himself thinking about the bed in the room, too. He knew gargoyles were stone during the day, so what did his sweet beloved use the bed for? Gripping the knob, Basques paused as a wave of jealousy crashed over him.

Sex was the obvious answer.

Except, that couldn't be right, since his sweet beloved had admitted to his inexperience.

Shaking his head at himself, Basques twisted the knob. The door opened, revealing a surprisingly small bathroom. He stepped inside and glanced around, taking in the utilitarian space.

The sink stood on the left, a single pedestal style with a medicine cabinet hanging over it. The toilet was next to it. A standard tub shower combo took up the right wall. Straight ahead was a door, which Basques assumed led to Praerna's closet and room. A hook was screwed into the wall between each door and the tub, presumably for hanging a towel while bathing.

Now the bathing items on the shelves in Dloben's closet made sense. While the bathroom appeared clean, it was small.

Basques really didn't like the picture he was seeing of Dloben's life at the clutch. Shaking his head, he returned to the closet and grabbed a couple of hand towels. As he soaked one with warm water, he wondered how long it would be until he convinced his sweet gargoyle to move to his coven.

His own suite was easily triple the size of Dloben's space and contained a private bathroom, a sitting room, a second bedroom he used as a personal office, and a small kitchenette.

While opening his pants and cleaning himself, Basques thought about all the fantastic things they could do in his en-suite's jetted tub. He smiled, rinsing the cloth. Draping it over the side of the sink, he dried himself using the second one, then after cleaning his pants, did them up.

While damp leather wasn't the most comfortable, it was better than having a crotch full of cum.

Basques then took both towels with him when he left, closing the door behind him. After grabbing a fresh loincloth for his lover, he took everything back to the bedroom. Spotting the empty bed, he frowned as he swept his gaze around the space.

There wasn't much to see — a bed, a nightstand with a lamp on it, a desk, and a chair.

Basques found his gargoyle standing at the door, accepting a tray from someone on the other side. Setting his items on the bed, he slowly crossed to him, making certain to make a humming noise of appreciation as he slid his attention over Dloben's backside. He didn't want to startle his skittish lover, after all.

Dloben peered at him as he used a foot to close the door. His cheeks flushed, and he glanced down at the floor only to peer at him shyly. He nibbled his bottom lip while offering Basques a tentative smile.

"Gods above, you're sexy," Basques whispered, enjoying the look. "How about you put that on the bed, so I can clean you up?"

Even though Dloben's blush deepened, he did as Basques had told him.

Basques knelt before Dloben. He noticed his little gargoyle's gasp of surprise and smiled up at him. "Let's make you more comfortable," he murmured, reaching for the stays of Dloben's loincloth. Just before pulling them, he met his beloved's gaze and asked, "May I?"

While the fact that the fabric was wet was hidden by the dark color, Basques could still smell the delicious scent of his gargoyle's spilled cum. His mouth watered. Holding Dloben's gaze, Basques waited.

"Y-Yes."

Grinning his pleasure, Basques quickly pulled the ties, then carefully peeled the soiled fabric from Dloben's groin. He groaned, dropping the loincloth to the floor as he took in the pale-blue hairless crotch before him. Dloben's slender penis hung half-hard before his face, the foreskin hiding his crown.

Spotting the white globs of seed on Dloben's flesh, Basques felt saliva pool in his mouth. His need to taste overruled every other hint of good sense. Leaning forward, he stuck out his tongue and lapped over Dloben's sack.

Dloben squeaked and jerked backward a step, nearly toppling onto the bed behind him.

Basques yanked his gaze away from the beautiful sight before him and peered up. Taking in Dloben's gaping expression, he didn't need his nose to realize he'd shocked the shit out of his small lover. He held his gargoyle's gaze as he gripped his gargoyle's slender hips. Leaning forward, Basques stuck out his tongue again.

When Basques swiped over Dloben's bobbing crown, a soft whine escaped the man. Loving that sound, he smiled and did it again. Licking his lips at the tasty treat, Basques went back for more.

Glancing between Dloben's face and his groin, Basques made quick work of licking his lover clean. During the process, his gargoyle's prick thickened and swelled. He hummed appreciatively as he grabbed the damp cloth and gently wiped it over his groin. When Basques wrapped it around Dloben's dick and jacked it, slow and gentle, he reveled in the way his gargoyle whined and bucked his hips.

"I love the way you respond to me, my beautiful gargoyle," Basques told him, teasing along his flesh. "May I suck you off?" Before Dloben could answer, he quickly added, "Be aware, it will start the bonding process."

Dloben's nostrils flared, and his eyes widened. "Y-You want to suck me?"

"More than anything," Basques answered honestly.

Furrowing his eyebrow ridges, Dloben mumbled, "B-But we h-haven't talked at all." He bucked into his hold as he gritted his teeth before blurting out, "You don't know anything about me."

Basques cocked his head as he ceased his movements. Releasing Dloben's dick, he set the towel aside as he rubbed over the ridges of his beloved's stomach. As he did that, he grabbed the dry towel and began rubbing him lightly.

"You are my beloved, Dloben," Basques stated, keeping his voice calm and reassuring. "It wouldn't matter if you were a whiney, bossy, snarky busybody. I would still want you." Seeing the way his gargoyle's jaw sagged open and his eyes widened, Basques grinned and waggled his brows. "Although, if that were the case, I suppose my lap and hand would get a workout as we sort through correcting that behavior."

Dloben cocked his head. "Lap and hand?"

Grinning broadly, Basques nodded. "Yep." He snickered upon seeing Dloben's confusion. "A naughty beloved would be put over my lap and spanked with my hand."

Gasping, Dloben once again jolted. That time his hip hit the bed hard enough for him to topple onto the comforter. He scrambled backward with eyes wider than Basques thought possible.

Realizing his mistake, Basques went on instinct. He lunged. As a vampire, he easily landed on the bed and sprawled over his lover.

"Shhhh," Basques purred, rubbing his hands over Dloben's sides, teasing at his beloved's wingskins. "You misunderstand, my sweet gargoyle."

Dloben trembled under his touch, and Basques reveled in the way his lover responded to his ministrations. Unfortunately, his words weren't nearly as pleasing. "You want to hit me," he cried, even as he humped under Basques. "No!"

Basques nuzzled Dloben's jaw, teasing kisses along his jawline. He struggled with how to explain. Deciding his gut was working fairly well so far, he nipped at Dloben's tendon, giving his gargoyle just a hint of pain but not enough to break his thick skin.

To Basques's relief, Dloben whined as the fragrance of his pre-cum filled the room.

"See how that causes pain, but you love the sensation?" Basques didn't give his beloved a chance to reply. "*That* is what spanking would be like to the bratty personality I described. They enjoy that kind of activity." Deciding to share a further truth, Basques admitted, "But it pleases me that you are not like that. I enjoy this kind of pleasuring so much more." Basques chuckled huskily as he nipped at Dloben's neck again. "Fate knows me so well."

Dloben stilled beneath him, and Basques lifted his head so he could sweep his gaze over his gargoyle's face. To his pleasure, he saw surprise and wonder in his lover's expression. Basques skimmed his fingertips along his jaw, pausing to tease at his lips.

"I do love the pain of your teeth on me," Dloben whispered his admission. "Does that make me weird?"

Basques quickly shook his head. "Of course not, my beloved. It's perfectly normal." Grinning widely, he admitted, "It draws out the anticipation . . . your desire to couple in such an intimate way, to feel our bond grow. I look forward to feeling your teeth in my neck, too."

CHAPTER SIX

Dloben calmed upon listening to Basques's explanation. Hearing the man threaten to spank him had sent him reeling, but the more he thought about it, the more he realized the vampire hadn't threatened to hit *him*. Basques had only been expressing how he would accept the beloved Fate had given him, regardless of their needs.

Lifting his hands, Dloben rubbed his blue fingers over Basques's light-brown hair. "Sorry I misunderstood," he murmured as he scraped his fingernails along the vampire's scalp.

"Forgiven," Basques murmured, his response immediate. He tipped his head and pushed into Dloben's caresses as his eyelids slid to half-mast. "Mmm, so good."

A surge of . . . something crashed through Dloben. As he continued to massage his vampire's head with his claws, he struggled with placing the sensation. When Basques rested his forehead on Dloben's chest and groaned softly, it hit him.

Pride.

Dloben's touch had reduced Basques to a puddle of relaxed goo, and he was damn proud of that fact.

I did this.

As much fun as it would be to see how long Basques would allow him to continue caressing him, the growling of his stomach interrupted the moment.

Chuckling softly, Basques lifted his head and pulled away. "Let's get you fed, my beloved, and while we eat, we will chat about our expectations for our bonding."

Dloben didn't quite know what to make of that comment,

but he nodded anyway. When Basques eased off of him and off the side of the bed, his vampire traced his fingertips down the side of his hip. The appreciative hum from the man reminded Dloben of his nudity, and he moved his hand to hide himself.

Basques gripped his wrist in a light hold, pulling his hand away. "No hiding from your mate," he ordered softly.

Sweeping his gaze over Basques's clothed form, Dloben blurted out, "Well, how come I have to be naked, if you're not?"

Offering Dloben a winning smile, Basques gripped the hem of his t-shirt. "Excellent idea." Then he whipped it over his head and tossed it to the foot of the bed. As Basques unbuttoned and unzipped his fly, he lowered his tone and reminded, "Just because I'm getting naked, it doesn't mean anything has to happen. This is us getting comfortable with each other."

Feeling tension he hadn't been aware of ease from his body, Dloben nodded. "Okay." He moved to a sitting position, tucking his legs under him and resting his hands on his knees. "Um, are you hungry, too?"

Dloben gripped the edge of the tray and pulled it closer. Flicking his gaze to Basques, to the tray, and back again, he finally landed his focus on the vampire's groin and his half-hard dick. His lips *oh*ed in surprise as he took in the huge piece of meat jutting from his groin.

Basques growled. "I do love the way you're looking at me, Dloben." Reaching out, he cradled Dloben's jaw and urged him to lift his chin and meet his gaze. The vampire appeared extremely pleased, his deep blue eyes twinkling with pleasure. "But food first, sweet, handsome gargoyle. And talk."

Dloben nodded a smidge as he licked his lips.

Moaning, Basques bent and pecked a kiss to his lips. Then

he released Dloben's chin. With a wink and an air of confidence that was sexy in and of itself, he sauntered around the bed, comfortable in his nudity.

Dloben didn't blame him, either. His vampire was absolutely drool-worthy. Between his deeply tanned features, pale-blue eyes, and strapping, heavily muscled body, Basques was a gorgeous specimen of maleness.

Adonis.

Unable to rip his gaze away from Basques, even as he removed the lids from the dishes on the platter, Dloben admired his lover.

Gods above. My lover!

Basques stood six-foot-four, sported broad shoulders and a trim waist, and sexy six-pack abdominals. His arms were ripped with muscle, and his thighs bulged even more. His light-brown chest hair matched that on his head, which covered his torso only to travel southward to his groin to cradle his huge prick. The hair there appeared shorter, betraying the fact that Basques was a groomer.

Huh.

"So, what's for supper, handsome?" Basques asked as he lifted his leg and settled next to him on the comforter. His gaze strayed to the food. "Mmm, fried chicken. Nice."

For a few seconds, Dloben could just stare. He took in the way Basques sat with one leg bent and the other stretched out before him. Resting his weight on his right hand, he appeared completely at ease . . . as if eating naked with a lover was completely normal.

Jealousy churned in his gut.

"Do you do this often?" The question popped out of his mouth before he could stop himself. He felt the heat flood his cheeks and knew he blushed. Hunching in on himself, he muttered, "Sorry."

Basques lifted his pierced right eyebrow.

How does a piercing on a huge bruiser of a man look sexy?

Dloben didn't know, but he found it so.

"Do you mean sit and eat naked with someone?"

Unable to find his tongue in his embarrassment, Dloben simply nodded.

Leaning toward Dloben, Basques stared at him with intense blue eyes. Once his face was only a couple of inches from Dloben's own, he whispered, "No." Then he bussed Dloben's mouth with his lips before straightening. "How's your clutch's cooking? They any good? What's your favorite piece?"

Then Basques grabbed an empty plate and set it on his upturned knee. Next, he snagged two pieces of fried chicken — a leg and a thigh. After taking the second plate, he placed a large breast on it.

Lifting one, then the other, Basques offered, "White meat or dark?"

"I like both," Dloben replied, trying to wrap his mind around Basques's simple answer. As he reached out and took the plate with the leg and thigh, he wondered, "So why are you so comfortable, then?"

Basques winked at him as he grabbed a wing and added it to his plate. "Because you're my beloved." Once again resting the plate on his knee, he grabbed the bowl of garlic mashed potatoes and held it up. "Want some?"

"Definitely." Holding out his plate, Dloben watched Basques plop a large dollop onto it. He hummed appreciatively. "I love this stuff."

Nodding, Basques commented, "Noted," as he took some for himself, then placed the bowl back on the platter. "I'm not certain what this is called," Basques admitted when he picked up another bowl.

Dloben swept his gaze over the contents and held up his plate again. "Broccoli salad." While Basques scooped some up and placed it on his plate, he told him, "It has broccoli, obviously, as well as bacon bits and cheese, and it's drizzled with Italian dressing."

Basques nodded. "Okay." Then he took some for himself.

Taking a bite of his thigh, Dloben crunched happily through the crispy-covered meat. He appreciated the flavors exploding across his tongue. Once he'd finished the piece, he placed the bones on his plate, then grabbed a napkin and wiped his fingers.

Next Dloben snagged a fork and scooped up some mashed potatoes. Alternating between them and the salad, he ate steadily, filling his stomach. Then he finished with the leg.

"So," Basques began after nearly ten minutes of quiet eating. "I'll be upfront and ask if you'd be willing to move to my coven to be with me." When Dloben's jaw froze while chewing the last of his chicken, Basques offered a kind smile. "I'm the head enforcer there. My coven relies on me."

Dloben knew that. He finished chewing and swallowing, then licked his fingers before wiping them clean again. Meeting Basques's gaze, he stared at the vampire as he forced his lips into a small smile.

"I get what you're saying," Dloben whispered. "And it's the most logical move."

That didn't mean it didn't terrify him — moving to a strange place with unknown people.

"You are my Fate-given beloved, Dloben," Basques reminded him. Reaching over, he rested his hand on his upper thigh, squeezing lightly. "To vampires, just as with your people, that bond is sacred. You will be safe there." As he held Dloben's gaze, his expression turned earnest. "I will offer you any opportunity I can. What will make you happy?"

Dloben set aside his plate and rested his hand over Basques's. His vampire flipped his hand, and Dloben threaded their fingers. He squeezed lightly.

"I don't really have any aspirations," Dloben admitted, shrugging. "I just want to be happy and loved." Recalling the job that he'd recently started within his clutch, Dloben asked, "Does your clutch, um, I mean coven" — he fought back a blush at his slip — "Do you all have a garden? I like to be outside."

The freedom of feeling the wind on his face and seeing the moon on his skin was something he truly enjoyed. It had been so rare to have it under Grecian's rule. He'd been stuck inside cooking and cleaning.

"We do have a garden," Basques confirmed, grinning. His deep blue eyes twinkled as he leaned closer. "I bet our gardener, Clinton, could use more help." Then his voice lowered, taking on a husky quality. "If you enjoy gardening now, in the dark, I bet you'll love it when you can feel the warmth of the sun on your skin."

A shiver worked through him, and Dloben nibbled his bottom lip.

"We would have to complete the claiming for that," Dloben whispered, a fresh wave of arousal causing butterflies to bounce around in his belly. He couldn't help but remind, "Chieftain Kinsey told you how that works for gargoyles."

Dloben watched Basques's jaw clench for a second. Then he swallowed hard enough to cause his Adam's apple to bob. Meeting Dloben's gaze, a wry smile curved his lips.

"I won't lie and tell you I look forward to your dick up my ass, handsome." Basques glanced pointedly at Dloben's groin, and where Dloben's erection had begun to flag with the vampire's declaration. "You're big, which is typical for a paranormal, and bottoming isn't really my thing, but I know it's the quickest way, and I want to give you whatever you need."

Dloben licked his lips once, twice, then said the only thing that he could. After all, he was a paranormal, and this man was his mate.

"Okay. I'll move in with you."

For a second, Basques just stared at him . . . as if uncertain of the words he'd just heard. Then his eyes widened, his lips curved into a broad grin, and his pleasure radiated from his expression. Basques grabbed Dloben's upper arms and tackled him to the bed.

After pressing a firm, hard kiss to Dloben's lips, Basques peered down at him and declared, "Thank you, handsome. You won't regret it. I promise."

Scenting the joy radiating from his vampire, Dloben knew, no matter how difficult the change would be, he'd made the right choice.

I hope.

CHAPTER SEVEN

A spike of anticipation and lust surged through Basques. *My little gargoyle agreed.*

Of course, that also meant giving up his own ass . . . something he hadn't done since first experimenting with sex when he was seventeen. Over two centuries was a long time. Still, he would do anything for his beloved.

"So . . ." Basques began, drawing the word out. As he spoke, he placed his plate on the tray before doing the same to Dloben's empty plate. "Are you ready to bond with me, my handsome beloved?" Stretching out on the bed, Basques smiled up at his still-sitting soon-to-be lover. "If you're not ready for that step, we'll just keep getting to know each other until you are."

Dloben nibbled his bottom lip while shifting uncomfortably on the bed. "But I'll have to roost during the day if we don't."

Basques rested one hand behind his head and placed the other on the small of Dloben's back. "Roost?" he asked curiously as he slid his hand up and down his gargoyle's spine. It pleased him when his lover pressed into his touch. "What's that?"

"It's what we call it when we turn into a stone statue during the day," Dloben told him, his tone lowering and taking on a husky note. "Even after we go through molt"—he glanced at him and, with a smile, explained—"that's what we call taking our human form for the first time."

After Basques had nodded his understanding, Dloben continued.

"Once we go through molt, then we can choose when we want to roost." Dloben's thick lips turned down into a worried frown as his gaze turned vacant. "Although we still have to do it at least once a week or our bodies will force the issue and do it for us, so —" He shrugged.

Basques understood. Having his lover turn to stone would always be a part of their lives. Teasing over a bump of Dloben's spine, Basques wondered, "Do you control the length of sleep while in stone form? Is there a way to set an alarm clock, like I would while sleeping?"

Dloben's pale-blue brow ridges furrowed. "I'm not sure. I'll have to talk to my chieftain."

Nodding, Basques accepted that. Then another thought struck. "You know, once you move, he won't really be your chieftain, right?" Upon seeing Dloben's expression turn confused, he added, "You will have to swear fealty to Master Krispin."

"Oh."

Dloben nibbled his bottom lip for a few seconds while he darted his gaze around the room. With his eyes narrowed, he rubbed the back of his neck. His scent expressed his unease, tainting his naturally pleasant aroma.

"Dloben," Basques murmured, rubbing his back more firmly, attempting to gain his beloved's attention. "What has you so distressed by that?"

Glancing Basques's way, then peering around again, Dloben inhaled deeply as his spine straightened. Finally, he focused on him and softly asked, "Is he a good master? F-Fair?"

Basques immediately nodded once more. "Oh, yes, Dloben," he reassured. "Krispin is a very good leader . . . and my friend. I have known him my whole life."

"Wow!" Dloben stared at him with wide eyes. "You said

you were two hundred thirty-eight, right?"

Pleased that Dloben had retained that detail, he grinned. "Yes. We grew up in the same coven, and when a new master took it over by force, we didn't like his ideals." Basques's smile slipped away as he growled under his breath. "Asshole was a bigoted specist."

"Specist? What do you mean?"

Basques huffed a sigh as he clenched the fingers of the hand under his head. "The vampire thought all other races were beneath vampires, and their one purpose was to feed us. Even had grand ideas of figuring out a way to rule all races." Rolling his eyes, he grumbled, "I hear he only lasted a few years as the master there before the council stepped in and removed him." Seeing Dloben's gaping mouth, Basques informed him, "Danger to the secrecy of all paranormals, you see."

"Right," Dloben whispered.

"Anyway, myself, Krispin, and Ridger were long gone by then." Basques shivered as he recalled those days. "We were named rogue by our ex-master, but we weren't really. While we could petition another coven to take us in, we faced a couple of problems." He couldn't help the growl that slipped into his voice as he continued to share his past and why he could so easily defend his friend. "After receiving refusals from all the nearby covens, we discovered our ex-master had bad-mouthed us, stating we were rogue because we'd attempted to deny his rightful claim of master when he took over and instead of challenging him honorably, we jumped him from behind. Not true, of course." Curving his lips in a sneer, Basques thought the lying asshat had gotten what he deserved—death from the hand of a council enforcer. "Eventually, we decided to form our own coven."

Basques paused, remembering those days. It had been difficult, having to decide if they were going to accept rogue vampires. Knowing that a person's history could be a lie, they had kept a watchful eye on everyone admitted and only accepted those alone.

They couldn't take any chances that by accepting a group, they could have been rousted from leadership.

Safety first.

"Anyway, that was about a hundred and fifty years ago, and we've made a good home together."

"If you're all best friends, how did you decide who would be the master, the second, and the head enforcer?"

Appreciating that his tale had calmed Dloben and brought out the gargoyle's curious side, Basques hummed. "It was an easy choice, actually," Basques told him. "Neither myself or Ridger have a true desire to lead. On top of that, Krispin is far more dominant than either of us. With our support, he can easily fight off attacks from others." Shaking his head, Basques added, "Which we did as we established the coven. Now we're pretty well respected."

"And the second and enforcer positions?"

Basques chuckled as he waggled his brows at his gargoyle. "Rock, paper, scissors."

Dloben's brow ridges shot up even as he nodded again. "Okay."

Sliding off the bed, Dloben swallowed hard enough that Basques noticed the way his Adam's apple bobbed. He grabbed the platter and headed to his desk chair. After setting it down, Dloben crossed to his nightstand.

He reached into the second drawer and pulled something out. With his back to Basques, he hid the object for a few heartbeats. Finally, he turned around and revealed he held a tube of lubricant.

"I know I told you I haven't ever done much with anyone, but that doesn't mean I haven't done things with myself." Dloben's blue skin took on a deep pinkish hue. Still, he forged ahead. "I have a tail, and I'm really good at controlling it. I —

" Finally, Dloben paused, appearing to struggle with his words.

The words were on the tip of Basques's tongue to ask about what kinds of things he did with his tail. Then it hit him. His pulse thundered through his veins as the sexy idea filled his imagination.

"Handsome gargoyle." Basques couldn't help the growl filling his words. "Do you fuck yourself with your tail?"

Dloben stopped nibbling his lower lip just long enough to nod once. "Yeah." He didn't stop there, however. "Y-You said you don't like to bottom, but I do. I like the stretch and burn of my tail." Absently rubbing his stomach, Dloben muttered, "I figure a dick will be different, but"—his gaze flicked to Basques's now-bobbing shaft, then focused on the comforter—"I bet I can still make it okay for you." His cheeks darkened as he whispered, "I hope."

"I would very much like for you to show me," Basques stated, his own voice turning husky. He barely resisted the urge to grip his dick. "Tell you what." Swallowing hard, Basques forced himself to continue. "Why don't we start with you coming over here so we can make out? Think you could play with my ass with your tail while doing it?"

Easing onto the bed, Dloben crawled toward him.

Basques reached for the gargoyle, the man who would complete him, and his blood pulsed through his veins. He swallowed the saliva pooling in his mouth as his anticipation of tasting his beloved caused his fangs to tingle. The hairs on his arms lifted, standing on end, as he gripped his little gargoyle's waist.

Never in his life had he felt such eagerness.

I found my beloved.

"Come here," Basques said on a growl. With his paranormal strength, he easily maneuvered Dloben into the position he wanted. He urged the small gargoyle to straddle his hips, giving him the ability to spread his own legs—not something he did . . . ever. To distract himself from the unfamiliar sub-missive move, Basques gripped the base of Dloben's neck and urged him to lever over him. "Love how you taste, beloved."

Then Basques guided Dloben's mouth to his own. He pressed their lips together, opening them and pressing his tongue to his gargoyle's. Thrusting into the other man's cav-ity, he took slow, thorough mastery.

Basques tangled his tongue with Dloben's, finding the sen-sation of the longer appendage against his own fascinating. He relished the whimper the move drew from the man. As Basques explored, he rubbed his hands up and down Dlo-ben's sides, using his hands on his beloved's wingskins to draw out more whimpers and moans.

When Dloben pressed his hard erection against Basques's stomach and began rocking, he palmed the man's ass and en-couraged the movement. He knew as a paranormal who'd just met his mate, Dloben would easily be able to get it up again. It also gave him the chance to knead and massage his gargoyle's delectable rear end.

The feel of the slightly harder mottled hide beneath his palms tantalized his nerve endings, and he couldn't wait to feel all his lover's flesh sliding against his own.

When breathing became a necessity, Basques slowly ended the kiss. Dloben's gasps for breath mirrored his own. When Basques teased the dock of his tail, his little gargoyle trembled and shuddered in his arms.

Oh, another hot spot.

Basques filed that away but didn't pursue it. Instead, he began lapping along the tendons of his neck as he murmured against Dloben's skin. "You want me to open the lube for you, beloved?" he crooned into his gargoyle's ear. "Pour that on your tail?"

There was no way Basques planned to take the appendage dry. It didn't matter how much control the gargoyle had over it. Plus, he wanted to get things moving in the right direction.

"Y-Yeah," Dloben muttered, holding up the tube that he'd been clutching. However, he didn't stop his rocking thrusts.

Basques took the offered item, sparing just enough attention to pop the cap as he continued to worship Dloben's tasty flesh. He sucked hard, pulling up a mark, reveling in his gargoyle's unique flavor. To his pleasure, his beloved held up his tail and waved it.

"Pour lube over the last several inches of the tip," Dloben ordered, his voice rough.

While Basques preferred to be the one in charge, he still obeyed. He drizzled plenty of the slick fluid over the appendage's end, then used his thumb to close the cap before setting the lube aside. Then he returned his hand to Dloben's ass, helping to encourage his lover's thrusts.

To Basques's surprise, just as he felt Dloben jolt in his arms and scented the sweet, earthy fragrance of his released cum, he noticed the teasing touch of something slender against his ass. Knowing it was his gargoyle's tail, he reminded himself not to clench. As he petted his blissed-out beloved, who lay sprawled on his chest, Basques pushed out and accepted the slender appendage into his chute.

"Mmmm," Dloben all but purred. "You're tight."

Basques swallowed hard as he felt his inner walls stretch. Keeping himself relaxed by taking slow even breaths, he used his fingers' movements over Dloben's skin to keep himself distracted. The stretch and burn wasn't much, but it reminded him why he preferred to top.

Dloben turned his head and peered up at Basques. His brow ridges were furrowed when he met his gaze. "You doing okay?"

Needing to reassure his lover, Basques nodded. "I'm okay." He lifted his head and gave his gargoyle an awkward kiss. "Just been a while." Then he forced a grin as he waggled his brows. "Give me more, handsome. I won't break."

Taking him at his word, Dloben eased more of his tail into Basques. The way the slender appendage twisted and turned inside him felt . . . strange. The walls of his channel were pressed here and there, setting his nerve endings on fire in a way Basques had never before experienced.

To Basques's surprise, he found his cock twitching with the sensations. When Dloben rubbed over his prostate, a moan was ripped from him.

"There it is," Dloben whispered. "Knew I'd find it." He grinned up at him, clearly pleased with himself. "What if I combine it with this?"

Then a low purring vocalization came from Dloben. While Basques found the noise itself soothing, it was the way Dloben vibrated just a little and rocked against his dick that sent his arousal soaring. It was as if the gargoyle had turned himself into a living vibrator . . . and he was rubbing his front all over Basques's cock while sending those same vibrations up his chute and over his prostate with his tail.

"Holy fuck!" Basques cried as his balls tightened so fast he couldn't hope to hold back his orgasm. "Dloben!"

His back arching, Basques came. His throbbing shaft pulsed, soaking the space between them, adding his mess to Dloben's. His senses reeled as the endorphins from his release swelled through him.

Basques barely registered it when Dloben eased his tail out of his body. Hearing the snick of the lube as his gargoyle shifted off of him, he opened one eyelid, although he didn't know when he'd even closed them. His body felt relaxed and sated, which was odd since his dick remained hard, as he watched Dloben slick up his shaft.

When Dloben guided his cock to Basques's hole, levering over him, his gut clenched. His gargoyle's erection was *so* much bigger than his tail. With that realization, he tensed.

"Easy, Basques," Dloben whispered, peering up at him. He

rubbed his palm over Basques's abdominals, petting and soothing. "We don't have to do this if you don't want to . . . if you're not ready."

Even as Basques felt a rush of gratitude upon hearing those words, the feeling was tempered by shame. His gargoyle planned to accept him next. How could he do less for his beloved?

"I want this," Basques declared. To his surprise, as he spoke the words, he realized they were true, too. Reaching up, Basques gripped Dloben's upper arms and rubbed up and down them as he held his lover's gaze. "I really do want this. Just . . . please go slow."

As much as it galled him to have to ask for that, Basques knew he always had to be honest with his beloved.

"I want to feel you, but I'm a bit worried about your size." Basques twisted his lips into a wry grin. "You're not exactly small."

From the looks of it, Dloben's dick was a good eight inches and had a hefty girth.

Dloben nodded as he nibbled his lower lip and searched Basques's gaze. "Okay. Tell me if it's too much."

Sliding a hand up to cradle Dloben's jaw, Basques nodded once. He crunched up and pressed a swift, hard kiss to his man's lips. "I will." Then he relaxed back on the bed and spread his legs a bit wider. "Do it, my beloved. Fill me."

CHAPTER EIGHT

Dloben nearly trembled with anticipation as he nodded while pushing forward. Even as he tried to peer at Basques's face to gauge his response, he found his focus riveted to where his flared crown pushed against the slicked, stretched ring. His wide head caused the muscle to spread, and between one heartbeat and the next, his cock disappeared inside the vampire's body.

The squeeze that clamped onto his dick's head yanked a whine from his throat. At the same time, his balls rolled, threatening to tighten. He sucked in a harsh breath as he froze, trying to stem his need to come.

"Push in, Dloben," Basques urged, a rasp filling his voice. "Come on, handsome. I'm okay."

Dloben opened his mouth, then closed it again. After swallowing to get moisture into his too-dry throat, he whispered, "T-Trying not to come."

Basques's husky rumble did nothing to help Dloben's control.

"You don't have to fight that urge, handsome beloved," Basques told him. Then lifting both legs, he wrapped them around Dloben's waist. "Push into me and come."

Digging his heels into Dloben's back while wrapping his arms around his torso, Basques forced him forward.

Dloben gasped as Basques's hot, tight channel swallowed him to the root. With a cry, he lost his balance and flopped over the vampire's broad, muscled torso. His hips jerked, pulling his cock partway out only to shove it back in deep.

With a whine, Dloben gave in to his body's impulse. He groaned roughly as his orgasm rocked through him. His dick spurted, and he trembled through the most intense release he'd ever experienced. Spots danced across his vision, and he panted hard to get enough air into his lungs.

"Claim me, beloved."

Basques's hot whisper against his hair caused Dloben's instincts to surge.

Opening his mouth, Dloben sank his teeth into the meaty flesh of Basques's pectoral, right above his heart. Due to their height differences, it was the highest he could reach. The vampire's blood oozed up around his teeth, filling his mouth.

Dloben moaned again as the sweet, iron-rich fluid coated the hundreds of receptors on his tongue. Wanting more, he sucked on Basques's flesh. To Dloben's pleasure, Basques groaned and shuddered beneath him.

The scent of Basques's seed flooded Dloben's senses anew.

Easing his teeth free, Dloben lapped at the wound. His teeth marks were deep, and between knowing his mate had come from his bite along with seeing his mark on the vampire, a surge of smug satisfaction filled him. Dloben cleaned up the remaining blood, sealing the wound.

"That'll leave a pretty scar," Dloben commented absently.

"Yes, it will." Basques used a finger under Dloben's chin to get him to lift his head enough to meet his gaze. The vampire's deep blue eyes danced with mirth and . . . something else. Satisfaction. "Like that, don't you?"

Dloben nodded, pride filling him.

Basques dipped his head and placed a kiss on his lips. "Me, too." Waggling his brows, he told him, "Loved how that felt. You can bite me anytime."

Grinning widely, Dloben nodded. "Okay."

"And now," Basques lowered his legs as he gently massaged Dloben's neck. His eyes narrowed as a feral light filled his gaze. "It's my turn."

With a skillful press and push with his legs and arms, Basques rolled them. The vampire grinned down at him as he eased upward to loom over Dloben. The move caused Dloben's semi-hard dick to slip from the warmth of the vampire's body, and he moaned as he held his mate's gaze.

Basques hummed as he lowered his head and nuzzled along the side of Dloben's neck. "Sorry about that," he whispered, licking along the tendon of his neck. "Got a little eager."

Dloben tipped his head, offering more room. "I-It's okay." He hummed, appreciating the stinging scrape of Basques's fangs along his neck. "I-I want t-to complete our—"

His thoughts left him when he felt Basques's knee push between his legs, nudging his balls. He immediately spread his legs, welcoming his lover between them. Next, he felt the teasing touch of a lubed finger against the sensitive muscle of his hole.

Dloben rocked his hips, chasing the light touch. "Pleeeease," he hissed.

A low growl rumbled from Basques's chest. "Gods, you're so responsive." He lifted onto his elbow and peered down at Dloben with red-irised eyes. "So gorgeous in your pleasure."

Blinking, Dloben cleared his lust-addled brain a little as he took in Basques's feral expression. "I-Is that, um . . . normal?" he couldn't help but ask as he stilled beneath his lover.

Basques grinned widely. "The red eyes?" After Dloben nodded, the vampire nodded back. "It is. Is it okay if I explain vampire traits later, beloved?"

Dloben took Basques at his word. "Yeah. If you say it's normal, then I believe you."

"Thank you."

Then Basques lowered his head and captured Dloben's mouth. He didn't ask. He conquered, dominating with his tongue, mapping, teasing, and licking.

At the same time, Basques pushed his finger all the way inside Dloben's chute. He wiggled his digit around, then pulled it out, replacing it with two. Crooking them, he rubbed Dloben's prostate.

Fire shot through Dloben's rectum, making him cry out into Basques's mouth. Basques returned the sound with a growl of his own. As Basques ate at Dloben's mouth, he clung to the vampire, his senses reeling with the stimulation.

When Basques finally broke the kiss, Dloben sucked in a harsh gasp. Maybe his senses had been reeling for a different reason . . . like lack of oxygen. Then Dloben met his lover's intense gaze while feeling the push of Basques's crown against his hole.

Dloben's heart pounded in his chest as he felt his ring stretch. He pushed out. Then his lover slipped inside him, ripping a moan from him upon the amazing sensation of connecting with his vampire.

"Oh, Dloben," Basques said on a growl, gripping the top of one of Dloben's braids and tugging gently. "You feel so fucking good." Rocking his hips, he began a slow thrust and retreat. "Love the way you look at me."

When Basques adjusted his angle, his next thrust rubbed across his prostate.

Dloben groaned, shivering as Basques's rhythm increased, and his vampire nailed his gland at every stroke. Blissful fire coursed through his veins. His senses sang, and his mind reeled.

Every little movement Basques made appeared to be geared toward driving him out of his ever-loving mind.

The vampire's hands seemed to be everywhere, tracking over his wingskins, tugging his nipples, and teasing his cock. Even the sting of his teeth over his neck tendon made his stomach flutter. His body felt as if it was going up in flames, and his dick throbbed with each beat of his heart.

"Come for me, pretty gargoyle," Basques urged as he began stroking his erection in earnest. "Paint our chests. Spray us with your pleasure."

Dloben could do nothing but obey. His body arched, his chute clenched, and his eyes practically rolled into the back of his head. He roared with bliss as his third orgasm in less than thirty minutes pulsed through his body.

Basques's deep groan, coupled with the warmth that suddenly flooded his chute, told Dloben that his vampire lover had found his own release. Trilling happily, he rubbed his cheek against his lover's. The scent of their sweat, semen, and natural musk filled the room, causing Dloben's senses to sing.

"You're gonna have to tell me what that noise is that you're making," Basques rumbled, his breath tickling his ear. "But later. Ready to come one more time?"

Dloben chuckled softly. "Don't think that's possible."

"It *is* possible," Basques countered. Then he moved his mouth to Dloben's neck. "Now."

Basques's fangs sank through Dloben's flesh. For an instant, he felt pain. Then that was replaced by the sweetest surge of fiery, tingling ecstasy.

Crying out once more, Dloben jerked, but Basques held him steady. Each sucking pull the vampire placed on his neck went straight to his groin. His cock swelled once more, and just as Basques had predicted, he shot.

His body bowing and shuddering, Dloben couldn't stop the darkness from descending.

Dloben slowly roused, his body feeling sated in a way he didn't know was possible. Stretching his arms, he moaned softly at the delicious aches in all the right places. When his hand landed against hard flesh, he snapped his eyes open.

Meeting Basques's deep, blue-eyed gaze, Dloben felt heat

rise to his cheeks.

Basques gripped Dloben's wrist and brought it to his mouth. "Welcome back, my love," he rumbled before placing a soft kiss to the pulse point on the inside of his wrist. "You honor me with your passion."

Smiling shyly at his lover, Dloben whispered, "You're honored because I passed out?"

"Oh, yes," Basques replied, rubbing along his stomach, then wrapping his arms around Dloben and pulling him close. "You were magnificent in your pleasure."

Dloben snuggled against Basques, simply deciding to accept what his lover said. After all, he smelled divine, telling him that the vampire believed his words. Sighing, Dloben rubbed his palm over Basques's stomach as he gently scraped the lines of his prominent six-pack abdominals with his claws.

"So . . . the eyes?" Dloben ventured. "Your irises were blood red, but now they're back to dark-blue."

Basques hummed as he traced his fingertips along Dloben's jaw. "A vampire's eyes turn red when they're going to fight or feed," he answered, obviously being blunt. "It turns my vision to something similar to infrared, giving me the ability to trace the blood pathways in someone."

"So you know where to bite or strike," Dloben mused.

Basques rubbed a couple of fingertips along his bone-spur as he nodded.

Dloben groaned when he felt his dick twitch. "Please, stop," he gasped, wriggling in Basques's grip. "I'm afraid if I get it up again, my dick will snap off."

Chuckling softly, Basques relented. "So. What about that vibrating thing you did?"

"It's called trilling," Dloben told him. Feeling his cheeks heat again, he admitted, "Normally it's used to calm an upset mate or friend, but um, I figured—" Pausing to clear his throat, Dloben tried to figure out the right words.

Basques didn't seem to need them. Grinning broadly, he waggled his eyebrows as he stated, "You figured why restrict it to that. Have you fucked yourself with your tail while trilling?"

Dloben nibbled his bottom lip as he felt his face go up in flames.

"Oh, Dloben," Basques crooned, nuzzling his jaw against Dloben's temple. "Don't be shy with me. I'm your beloved." Then he lowered his voice to a sexy rumble and claimed, "Besides, I love your creativity and can't wait to feel it again."

"Really?" Dloben couldn't hide his surprise. Basques hadn't seemed interested in bottoming.

Grinning, Basques told him, "You weren't kidding when you said you had great control over your tail. It felt fantastic, my beloved."

"Okay."

Basques rubbed along Dloben's braids as he peered down at him with a fond gleam in his eyes. "I love that even after everything we just did together, you still blush."

That only made Dloben's cheeks heat some more.

"Yes, just like that, my beloved." Basques turned his head and bussed a kiss over Dloben's warm cheeks. "Just like that." When he straightened, he stated, "Oh, another vampire fact. We should end up with the ability to speak in each other's minds."

"Like telepathy?"

Basques nodded. "Exactly. That way if you ever need me and I'm not around, you can contact me." As he relaxed on the bed, he claimed, "Better than any telephone."

"Huh. Okay." Dloben really didn't have anything to say to that. Except . . . wait—"Does that mean you'll be able to read my mind?" That could end up uncomfortable at times. There was a reason people didn't blurt out every thought that entered their mind . . . well, most people didn't, anyway.

"No," Basques assured, rubbing along his spine soothingly, having obviously scented his unease. "I'll only hear thoughts you project to me. We'll practice."

Dloben wasn't certain what to expect, and even when it happened, he still jerked in Basques's arms.

Can you hear me, handsome?

"Wow," Dloben whispered. "Yeah."

Basques's voice had rung through his head, clear as if he'd been speaking out loud.

Good. Now think up something random, and mentally will me to hear it.

Dloben paused for a moment, racking his brain for something appropriate. Finally, he decided on what to share.

Irises are my favorite flower.

Smiling, Basques stared back at him.

I prefer lilies, but irises are pretty, too. Now I know what kind of flowers to buy when I fuck up.

Gaping, Dloben forgot to respond mentally. "Fuck up? Fuck up what?"

"Our relationship," Basques replied as blunt as ever.

Dloben found it refreshing.

Basques cradled Dloben's face, using his thumb to rub his jaw line. "I'm an over two hundred-year-old vampire that has never been in a relationship before." His expression turned wry as he admitted, "I'm bound to screw up sometime." Then he winked as he pulled Dloben over to straddle his chest. "But I hear make-up sex is amazing."

Then Basques captured Dloben's mouth. For several long minutes, his vampire licked and lapped languorously. He kept the kiss slow and light, a comfortable meeting of lips and tongue.

Dloben was just beginning to feel his arousal begin to burn through his blood again when Basques ended the kiss. After rubbing their noses together, the vampire sighed. He relaxed his head on the mattress and smiled at Dloben.

"I suppose we should track down Chieftain Kinsey and tell him I'm moving," Dloben murmured, smiling up at his lover.

Gods. I have a lover. A mate.

That knowledge hit him all over again, and he sighed as he snuggled on Basques.

Wow!

"You're mine," Dloben whispered, a need to say the words rushing through him.

"Yes." Basques's response was immediate. "Yes, I am. Just as you are mine."

Filled with delight, Dloben leaned forward and kissed Basques once more.

Before he gave in to his sudden fresh rush of arousal, Dloben pulled away and slipped off the bed. "Come on. Let's shower and—" He paused, glancing down at himself. That was about the time he realized his skin had already been cleaned. "Oh."

Basques chuckled as he swung his legs over the side of the bed. "Washed you up while you were passed out. We can still shower, if you'd like."

Dloben nibbled his bottom lip uncertainly. "I kinda like having your scent on me," he admitted, rubbing his upper arms with his opposite hands. "You smell good."

Grinning, Basques wrapped his arms around Dloben. "While you will always smell of me, since we've claimed each other, I'm happy to intensify that smell any time you want."

With his cheek pressed against Basques's pectoral allowing him to eye his claiming mark, Dloben grinned. "Okay."

Basques barked a laugh as he swatted Dloben's butt, giving him a light smack. "Come on, my beloved. Let's go share our good news with your chieftain . . . then we'll track down Ridger and the other vampires." Pulling away, he explained, "They'll help us pack up your stuff."

"I don't have much," Dloben admitted as he picked up the clean loincloth Basques had grabbed for him and tied it into place.

After buttoning his leather pants, Basques wincing in the process, he stated absently, "Then it won't take us long." He slid his thumbs into his waistband and adjusted his pants. Upon seeing Dloben watching him, Basques curved his lips into a wry smile. "They're a little stiff, but at least the cum didn't soak through and make a spot."

Dloben bit his lip, fighting back a laugh as he remembered how they'd both come in their clothes not long ago.

Basques smirked as he tugged on his black t-shirt. "Har, har. I see that smile."

Slapping his hand over his mouth, Dloben let out a giggle. "Sorry," he said around another laugh. "Does it make me mean that I love how worked up I made you?"

Grabbing Dloben, Basques pecked his lips. "Not at all." His expression turned wicked as he peered down at Dloben. "After all, you came in your loincloth, so we were even."

Dloben blushed . . . again.

It was Basques's turn to laugh. Then he kissed Dloben again before releasing him and pulling on his socks and boots. Finally, he straightened and started toward the door, wrapping his arm around Dloben's waist to get him to walk beside him.

When they reached the door, Basques pulled it open, except the trill of a phone made the vampire pause. He slapped the back pocket of his pants, then frowned. "That's my master's ring tone," he explained as he glanced around. "Where— ah. Must have fallen out of my pocket when I shucked my pants."

Basques crossed to the bed and grabbed the device, answering the call in the process. At the same time, he waved his hand, silently telling Dloben to go ahead. As Basques greeted Master Krispin, he headed toward him.

Dloben exited his room and turned to the right, strolling

down the hall. Glancing over his shoulder, he saw the smile on Basques's face as he told his vampire master that they'd completed the bonding. As he turned the corner, Dloben saw Basques pause, reach back, and checked that his door was locked.

A tight grip on Dloben's upper arm had his attention snapping forward again. He barely managed a squeak of surprise before a hand came over his mouth. Then he was yanked into a nearby room, the slamming of the door telling him he was shut in with . . . whoever.

The other male released his hold and shoved Dloben into the wall.

After catching himself on his hands, Dloben spun to face his attacker. His heartrate spiked, and fear stabbed through him.

Chasis stared at him with hatred in his dark-brown eyes.

"Your lies had me reassigned to *cleaning* duty," Chasis snarled, curling his lip into a fierce expression. He clenched his hands into fists as he stalked toward Dloben. "I think you need a lesson to remind you of your place."

Cringing, Dloben tried to twist away from Chasis's striking right hand, but he wasn't completely successful. Pain stabbed through his side. As Dloben lifted his hands defensively, trying to ward off Chasis's next blow, he remembered his bond.

Basques!

CHAPTER NINE

"Yes, Master Krispin, Dloben understands my position, and he's agreed to move to the coven."

Basques couldn't keep the grin off his face, nor the pleasure out of his voice. He was the first within his coven to find his beloved in over fifty years. It was a good omen for the coven. Perhaps Fate was finally going to smile down on them.

"I'm glad to hear it, Bas," Krispin replied, his tone full of warmth. "I can't wait to meet your gargoyle. Is he going to want a position with enforcement or tracking?"

Even though Basques knew why his master would assume such a thing, he still chuckled as he answered in the negative. After all, he hadn't met any small gargoyles before that evening. The prior chieftain had made it seem all gargoyles were behemoths.

Gods, has it really only been a few hours?

"Hmmm . . . why do you find it funny that I would think your beloved would want a position of status," Krispin asked curiously. "If I recall correctly, gargoyles have a better sense of smell than vampires due to the extra receptors they have on their tongue."

Basques had forgotten about that. "Well, as it turns out, there are two kinds of gargoyles, and the second ones are quite a bit smaller." Humming, he added, "It's possible he might want to learn to be a tracker. I'll ask Dloben if that's something he'd be interested in. We're still getting to know each other," he told his master. "I know he enjoys gardening, so I'd planned to ask you if Clinton needed any help."

"Huh. Smaller?" Krispin's interest shown through loud and clear. "How much smaller?"

Pausing, Basques tried to find the words to explain the differences. "Well—"

Basques!

Dloben's panicked voice echoed through Basques's mind, causing his heartrate to spike and his pulse to pound. "Gotta go." Without another word to his master, he disconnected the call.

Sprinting around the corner, Basques shoved the phone into his back pocket. He skidded to a stop, surprised to find the hallway empty. Inhaling deeply, he growled upon scenting Dloben's fear . . . as well as the smell of another gargoyle.

Where the fuck is he?

Basques's eyes hazed as he followed the scent trail left behind by his beloved. Snarling deep in his throat, he didn't care for how the strange gargoyle's smell intertwined with Dloben's. Stopping at a door, Basques reached for the handle.

Locked.

The rule of the coven was to never go into a locked suite uninvited, so he assumed it was the same for the clutch, causing him to hesitate.

Then Basques heard a cry from within. His heart skipped a beat as he recognized Dloben's voice . . . and it was filled with pain.

Basques broke the rule.

With a roar, Basques lifted his booted foot and slammed it into the door close to the lock. The wood splintered and gave way under the force of his vampiric strength. Stalking forward, he took in the scene, and his claws slid from his nails.

"Whoever the fuck you are, get out of here," the huge gray gargoyle ordered, tossing Dloben in the direction of the wall while releasing the grip he'd had on his upper arm. "You don't want any of what this lying sub-species is getting."

Basques cast a quick glance Dloben's way, and a fresh

wave of rage crashed through him. His sweet gargoyle had a split lip, his eye was starting to swell, and he kept his left arm tucked to his side. Not to mention the thick, cloying scent of fear and rage permeated the room.

"You have attacked my beloved," Basques stated, then he lunged.

Whether in response to his words or his move, the gargoyle attacker froze. Basques took advantage. He slashed the claws of his right hand across the gargoyle's pectorals, then followed that up with a swipe across his belly.

The first strike left behind four satisfyingly deep wells. The gargoyle managed to mostly dodge the second by spreading his wings and flapping them. The move launched himself backward, which caused Basques's belly-swipe to leave only the slightest streaks of blood behind.

As soon as the gargoyle landed, Basques attacked again. He ducked under the slightly taller male's strike, spinning in the process. Slipping beneath the gargoyle's left wing, he slashed both clawed hands, tearing into the big, black appendage.

The gargoyle roared his anger as he spun, using his right wing as a battering ram.

Basques barely evaded the blow that would have knocked him on his ass if it had connected solidly. As it was, with the leathery folds of skin sliding along his upper back as he pivoted under it, his head still received a good whap. Ignoring the ringing in his ears, Basques faced off against his beloved's attacker again.

Searching for an opening, Basques assessed the male. He was a good three inches taller than himself and heavily muscled. While the gargoyle's thick gray hide offered him a modicum of protection, Basques could counter that with his vampiric speed. He guessed under normal circumstances — as in fighting outside — the male would have used his flight to his advantage.

In a bedroom, however, the odds were in Basques's favor.

Just as Basques shoulder-rolled to the male's right, slicing his claws into the back of the creature's calf as he turned, he heard a shout from the doorway. He ignored that in favor of rolling to his feet and pivoting to face his opponent once again.

Strong arms wrapped around Basques from behind, trapping his arms against his sides. He bent his elbows, intending to slice into the deep green, thickly muscled arms holding him. The sound of Second Destrawn's voice made him still.

"Settle down, Basques," the second ordered. "And tell me what the hell is going on."

"That blasted vampire attacked me," Chasis claimed, pointing at him. "I want him punished." He glanced at his wing and the blood dripping from his shredded appendage pointedly, then sneered at Basques. "A whipping. That'd be fitting for wing-shredding, right?"

Second Destrawn loosened his hold, but Basques knew better than to lunge at the asshole again. Instead, he used his words. "Perhaps it is *you* who should be whipped for attacking my beloved." He tapped the second's upper arm, then pointed at Dloben, who still rested on his ass against the wall, looking dazed.

"Your beloved?" the gray gargoyle repeated, a sneer in his tone. "That second-class gargoyle doesn't have a mate. Fate would never—"

"Gods above, shut up, Chasis," Second Destrawn snapped, releasing his grip on Basques. "Go to your mate, Enforcer Basques. I will take Chasis to the cells, then track down Chieftain Kinsey and find you in the infirmary."

"Thank you," Basques stated.

At the same time, Chasis roared, "What the fuck?"

Second Destrawn grabbed Chasis's bicep and used the

hold to swing him around. He locked the big gargoyle's arm behind his back. Holding it there with one hand, he used his other to grip the top of Chasis's good wing.

"That vampire is Dloben's beloved, so he's well within his right to protect his mate," Second Destrawn stated as he started the other male moving. "What excuse are you going to use for attacking him this time?"

Basques growled low in his throat, hating hearing that this wasn't the first time Chasis has attacked Dloben. Then the name clicked. "He's the bastard who still gives the smaller gargoyles a hard time. Him and Ducine." He glanced around as if expecting another gargoyle to appear, but he didn't scent anyone else in the room. "Was he part of this?"

"I'll find out," the second vowed even as Chasis peered over his shoulder and snarled at Basques.

Dropping to his knees beside Dloben, Basques dismissed the pair that were disappearing out the door. "Hey, Dloben," he crooned, keeping his voice low and soothing. Carefully reaching for his lover, he hated the way his man twitched and cringed away from him when he rested his hand on his gargoyle's shoulder. He massaged his man lightly as he urged, "Dloben, look at me."

Finally, Dloben snapped his focus to Basques.

Basques cupped his gargoyle's jaw in a gentle hold. "Hey, beautiful." Dipping his head, he carefully licked his tongue over his lover's split lip. Even though Dloben tensed, he didn't pull away, pleasing Basques. "One more swipe and it'll be healed."

As he did just that, he wished he could do more for the rest of his sweetheart's injuries. Unfortunately, a vampire's healing saliva — normally used to close the fang wounds left from their bite — couldn't heal bruising. That type of injury was internal . . . under the skin.

"Can you focus on me, Dloben?" Basques asked, disliking

the slightly glazed look on his gargoyle's face. "Come on. Look at me."

After a few more blinks, Dloben's eyes snapped to focus on Basques. "Basques," he mumbled on a gasp. Then he glanced around as fear filled his gaze. "Where —"

"Easy, my beloved. You are safe," Basques assured, gently turning his man's focus back to him. Upon seeing the questions in Dloben's eyes, he offered his gargoyle a sad smile. "I'm sorry he caught you alone in the hall. It will never happen again."

"You heard me?"

Basques nodded. "I heard you."

Dloben rolled to his knees, then sprung himself into Basques's arms. "You came for me."

"I will *always* come for you," Basques vowed, barely resisting the urge to hold his lover tight to his chest. He didn't want to hurt the man, so he rubbed up and down his spine, instead. "Although I'd really prefer this sort of thing doesn't happen again." Tracking over the bruising already forming around Dloben's eye, he growled, "I wanna kick his ass again for this."

Dloben snickered as he peered up at him while pressing into his hold. "You kicked his ass?"

"Hell yeah, I did."

"Wish I could have seen that." Then Dloben's brow ridges furrowed. "Maybe not. I would have been scared for you the whole time."

Basques didn't point out that Dloben had been in the room when it had happened, so he had indeed seen it. He just hadn't been coherent for it. That wasn't a nice thought.

"Okay, handsome. Let's get you to the doc, huh?" Basques slowly rose to his feet, never allowing Dloben to leave his arms. Instead, he just adjusted his hold so he cradled him to his chest as he headed out of the suite. "Can you tell me which way?"

"To the left." Dloben pointed.

Following Dloben's directions, Basques found the infirmary. He pushed through the swinging door and found himself in a waiting area. There was no one at the reception desk, so he eased Dloben onto a cushioned chair.

Basques strode to the desk and tapped the bell. Even before it had stopped ringing, a slender, winged gargoyle with pale reddish-yellow skin hustled into the room. The male appeared harried and frustrated. He tipped his chin in Basques's direction before crossing and kneeling before Dloben.

"Oh, Dloben," the doctor muttered, reaching for his hand. "Which asshole did this to you this time?"

"Chasis," Dloben murmured.

The doctor seemed surprised that Dloben replied.

Dloben, however, then smiled over at Basques and stated, "But my mate found me and stopped him."

"Mate?" The doctor turned his attention to Basques, who had crossed to sit beside Dloben. "Really?" Then he inhaled deeply, and his eyes widened even more. "I see." The doctor's eyes narrowed. "Will you be a good mate to Dloben?"

While surprised at the blunt question, Basques still nodded, finding respect for the gargoyle doctor budding inside him. "Dloben's happiness and safety are my main concern," he stated gruffly. "Imagine my surprise that as soon as I take a phone call, my beloved is attacked." Basques growled low in his throat before saying, "We will not be staying here. Dloben deserves a safe place."

The doctor nodded even as he sighed. "Chieftain Kinsey is trying, but some are slow to change."

"Then he needs to knock some heads," Basques snapped, angry all over again that his sweet beloved had been targeted by an asshole.

Sighing, the doctor began to nod.

"I'll have to keep your advice in mind, Enforcer Basques," Chieftain Kinsey stated, his voice announcing his presence as he pushed open the swinging doors. "But in the meantime, Doctor Cantral, can you tell me how Dloben is?"

"They just arrived," the doc, Cantral, told the chieftain. "Can you stand, young one?"

Basques returned to his feet. In what was probably a rude move, he brushed aside the doctor and scooped Dloben back in his arms. Unfortunately, seeing another male kneeling at his beloved's feet was starting to piss him off.

"Which room?"

Doctor Cantral bounced to his clawed feet, headed to the second door on the right, and pushed it open.

As Basques followed him, Dloben whispered, "You're being territorial."

"Yes, I am." Basques wasn't going to lie to his beloved. Smiling at him, he told him, "I'm sorry, handsome, but we're newly bonded, and I just found some asshole beating the shit out of you. I'm gonna be a bit over-protective for a bit."

Dloben beamed up at him. "I like it."

Sighing with relief, Basques pecked a kiss to Dloben's lips. "I'm glad."

Then Basques maneuvered them into the room and placed his gargoyle on the single-sized bed. With the headboard against a wall, there was plenty of space to work on either side of the mattress. Taking Dloben's hand, Basques stood steadfastly beside the bed.

Doctor Cantral began a quick examination, pressing here and there, asking if he hurt and how much.

Basques gritted his teeth as he listened to his beloved's hisses and watched his winces. Taking the call from his master had caused him to lag behind just enough for that asshole to get his hands on his sweet Dloben. The urge to rip Chasis's wings from his sockets surged through him, and he had to force down the growl.

Once Doctor Cantral finished his exam, he advised rest, fluids, and a topical cream to help with pain and stiffness. Straightening, the doctor focused a frown on Chieftain Kinsey, who'd been standing just inside the doorway the entire time, waiting silently. The doc crossed his arms over his lean torso.

"So, you have witnesses this time," Cantral stated, his tone containing a clear note of belligerence. "You gonna kick out those assholes?"

Chieftain Kinsey growled low in his throat as he scowled at Cantral. "Watch your tone, Cantral," he warned, but left it at that since he immediately added, "And I need Dloben and Basques's statement, so I can decide appropriate action." Then Kinsey focused on Basques. "And restitution." Crossing the room, he stopped on the other side of the mattress. "Dloben, what happened?"

Dloben nibbled his bottom lip as he glanced Basques's way.

Basques mentally preened that his gargoyle deferred to him. Nodding encouragingly, he urged, "Tell them what happened, my beloved."

So Dloben did, explaining how he'd been grabbed and what Chasis had said to him before he'd been viciously attacked. "And I don't remember much after seeing the door crash open, because Chasis slammed my head into the wall."

"That was me who kicked the door in," Basques picked up the story when Dloben fell silent. "I was kicking Chasis's ass until Second Destrawn put a stop to it."

Heaving a sigh, Chieftain Kinsey ran his clawed hand through his hair. "I'm sorry he attacked you, Dloben," he began, but a commotion outside the room drew his attention. "Shit, Sethnos," Kinsey said as he turned and headed out of the room. "What happened to Destrawn?"

"Not sure," Sethnos replied, his voice carrying through the open door. "I found him knocked out in one of the hallways."

After squeezing a worried-looking Dloben's hand, Basques released him and crossed to the door. He spotted Destrawn being half-carried, half-dragged by the gargoyle enforcer. Blood dribbled down the second's temple, and the male's eyes appeared glazed.

Doctor Cantral was at Destrawn's other side in an instant, slotting up beneath his opposite arm and guiding them toward another open doorway.

Perhaps hearing his chieftain's voice roused Destrawn, for he lifted his head and peered blearily at Kinsey. His words were slightly slurred, but Basques could still understand them.

"Ducine attacked me from behind while I was taking Chasis to the cells. He had a metal pipe. I don't remember much after he hit me on the head."

Chieftain Kinsey roared his anger as he stalked from the room. "Take care of him, Doc," he ordered, then beckoned to Sethnos. "You're with me. We have some tracking to do."

While Doctor Cantral took Destrawn's weight and disappeared into what must have been another exam room, Second Ridger, Carmine, and Kraymer arrived.

A sense of relief flooded Basques as he greeted the other vampires. It was time to get the hell out of the clutch. Even as he thought those words, Basques would be sure to find out what became of those assholes.

He never wanted to see his beloved injured again.

CHAPTER TEN

Dloben peered up at the towering structure. The entrance heralded it *The Clearmont Hotel & Suites*, but Basques had explained that only the first dozen floors were actually rooms. The thirteenth floor was dominated by a half dozen suites and offices, all utilized by the inner circle.

Master Krispin had set it up that way so he could stand as the first line of defense between his people and the outside world. The floor above that was security, and above them was the rest of the coven.

The formation had surprised Dloben. He would have thought that the master would have chosen the top floor for views and the prestige of living in a penthouse suite. Dloben found the master's dedication to his people impressive.

Of course, then Basques had explained that Krispin had it set up that way for a second reason. If there was any dissension within the coven, once discovered, they wouldn't be able to get away. The guarding of the structure went both ways.

Even though Basques had wanted to get on the road immediately, Dloben had convinced him to wait until sunrise. That way, Dloben could go through molt, and they wouldn't have to sneak into the coven, seeing as it was in a city. Dloben had loved watching the sun rise that morning, especially since he'd been curled up in the arms of his vampire.

They'd sat together on the roof as if having a picnic. Since physical contact with his mate dulled the pain of transformation, they'd both been naked. Basques had curled around Dloben as he'd changed, doing his best to stroke every bit of skin he could.

After that, they'd made love once more.

Hours later, Dloben watched out the window as Second Ridger drove the SUV into an underground parking garage. He stopped near a private elevator. Turning in his seat, Ridger smiled back at them.

"Welcome home, Dloben."

Feeling his cheeks heat a little, Dloben returned the vampire's smile. "Thank you."

Dloben had been surprised—pleasantly so—by the acceptance of all three vampires. They were all extremely pleased that Basques had found his forever love, treating him with respect. Carmine had even offered to find out how Dloben could help out their gardener.

Basques had reminded Dloben that he would need a couple more days of healing. While gargoyles had swift healing, it didn't happen overnight. Unfortunately, Chasis had gotten in some good licks.

Dloben didn't bother to tell Basques that he'd had far worse and still had needed to complete his chores for the clutch.

Once in the elevator, Dloben stared at his reflection. He rubbed up and down his t-shirt-clad arms. His vampire assured him that he found him attractive in both forms, but seeing himself in a human frame would definitely take some getting used to.

Dloben stood five-foot-eight, having lost a couple of inches. From others who'd gone through molt, he knew that was normal. His frame was slender but strong-looking, and he still had green eyes while his hair had taken on just a hint of color. It made him appear to have bleach-blond locks tumbling over his shoulders.

Basques slid his arm around Dloben's shoulders, teasing

his fingers through his hair where it hung over his shoulder. His mate had talked him into leaving it unbraided, and he was taking advantage. Dloben didn't mind, though, because he loved how his vampire seemed to want to touch him constantly.

When the elevator began ascending, Dloben gasped and pressed closer to Basques's side.

As his arm lowered to around Dloben's waist, Basques dipped his head and murmured, "Everything okay, beloved?"

"Never been in an elevator before," Dloben whispered back, which was kind of silly, since he knew the others would still easily be able to hear him.

Dloben glanced at the other vampires, but no disdain appeared on their features. Instead, he noticed a slight furrowing of Carmine's brows. Kraymer stared at his shoes, and Ridger met his gaze in the mirror and offered him a kind smile.

"Have you ever been away from your clutch before?" Basques asked, rubbing up and down Dloben's back.

Tipping his head, Dloben met Basques's gaze as he shook his head. "It wasn't done."

"Because you were a smaller breed of gargoyle?" Second Ridger asked, shoving his hands into the pockets of his jeans.

Dloben nodded. "There were a couple that transferred to other clutches, like Kinsey's older brother, Conchlin, but Chieftain Grecian put a stop to anyone else doing it." Sneering, he muttered, "Didn't like losing control of anyone."

"Sounds like a real asshole," Kraymer muttered.

"He was," Dloben replied softly, feeling the urge to glance around as if someone loyal to the gargoyle would pop out of the wall and punish him.

Basques must have picked up on his predicament, for he wrapped both arms around him and pulled him in tight.

"You're safe," he assured as he nuzzled Dloben's temple with his goatee.

Dloben was really coming to like how that felt. As much as he wanted to turn in Basques's arms and kiss his vampire, he didn't feel comfortable doing that with so many onlookers. His mate didn't seem to have the same hang-up.

Basques slid one hand up and cradled his jaw, rubbing his thumb under his bottom lip. He used the hold to urge Dloben to tip his head back. Then Basques sealed his lips over Dloben's own.

The kiss was light, chaste, and yet it still set Dloben's blood on fire. It also calmed his nerves.

The ding of the elevator registered to Dloben, but Basques didn't stop.

Instead, it took a deep, amused chuckle and a stranger's voice saying, "Welcome back, Enforcer Basques. I'm very happy for you."

Basques drew the kiss to an end and lifted his head, grinning at the stranger. "Thank you, Master Krispin." He indicated him, saying, "This is my beloved, the gargoyle, Dloben."

Master Krispin's blue eyes contrasted his short, black hair and deeply tanned features. Dloben would have thought the man hard, what with the firm jaw and tight lines around his thin lips. Instead, the twinkle in his pale eyes softened his expression.

"So I gathered." There was a teasing note in Master Krispin's voice. Stepping backward, he beckoned, "Would you care to step out of the elevator, so I can welcome him to the coven properly?"

Dloben felt his cheeks flush hotly as he realized the other men had already exited the space. Second Ridger stood close, using an arm to keep the elevator doors from closing. The other two stood behind the master, grins on their faces.

Basques chuckled as he guided Dloben out of the elevator. "Right."

Master Krispin held out his hand to Dloben. "It's a pleasure to meet you, Dloben." As Dloben took the vampire master's hand and shook, the male added, "Basques tells me that you enjoy gardening. Our hotel has an excellent indoor arboretum." Krispin winked before teasing, "Make certain Basques lets you out of the bedroom long enough to tour it."

While the others, even Basques, chuckled, Dloben felt his face heat. He ducked his head and shifted his feet. The vampire master was unlike any leader he'd ever met before. Of course, he'd only met two.

Humming, Master Krispin beckoned. "I see I've made you uncomfortable." His smile relaxed his chiseled features. "Come to my study, everyone, so I can introduce Dloben to the rest of the inner circle."

To Dloben's surprise, Basques tensed beside him. He learned soon enough why that was. As soon as he walked into the office, Dloben scented it — disdain.

Dloben cast a swift glance around the room. He spotted two others — one man and one woman. The man sported an interested expression as he stared back at him. The woman, on the other hand, she eyed him with clear distaste, as if Dloben were something that she'd scraped off the bottom of her shoe.

Basques probably saw it, too, for he headed to the opposite side of the massive office. After reaching a small sofa, he settled onto it and pulled Dloben down beside him. He kept his arm around his shoulders, tucking him close to his side. The others chose seats, filling the room nearly to capacity.

Master Krispin swept into the room, his stride sure as he rounded the desk and settled behind the oak behemoth. "Everyone, I would like you to introduce you to Dloben." Gone were the twinkling blue eyes and friendly tones. Instead, he spoke with a calm serenity. "Enforcer Basques has been blessed to find his beloved."

As nearly everyone offered congratulations, the woman scoffed.

Arching his left brow imperiously, Master Krispin pinned his gaze on her. "Do you have something to say, Tabatha?"

"No," she replied, although her tone held belligerence.

Master Krispin narrowed his eyes. "Really? Because that's not what your scent is telling the rest of us." He waved his hand in a *let's hear it* motion. "Come now. If you have concerns, I want to hear them."

With a huff, Tabatha rolled her eyes. "Look. You all know I don't have a problem with gay men, so don't take it like that," she began. Then her lip curled as she frowned at Dloben. "But really? *Him*? A creature like *that*?" Tabatha pointed at him. "He's unnatural."

Basques growled softly where he sat beside him. "Watch it, Enforcer Tabatha," he snarled. "You're talking about my gift from Fate."

Tabatha scoffed. "You all believe in that Fate crap?" She must have noticed that all the men in the room were frowning at her. Throwing her hands in the air, Tabatha had the gall—or stupidity—to continue sharing her opinions. "Come on, guys. You can't truly be okay with the idea of getting pregnant." Smirking at Basques, she asked, "I know gargoyles come from eggs. You gonna lay an egg for him like some kind of chicken?" She shuddered as if the very idea was abhorrent to her.

Master Krispin asked coldly, "Are you telling me that you cannot support Basques's bonding with his beloved?"

With her mouth open, Tabatha paused. She glanced around at the others, as if expecting one of them to support her views. After closing her mouth, she clenched her jaw hard enough that a muscle ticked in it.

"That is a yes or no question, Tabatha," the master pointed out, clearly expecting a response.

Dloben thought the absence of her title was conspicuous.

"If it is your wish, I will accept it," the female enforcer replied.

Unable to help himself, Dloben opened his mouth and scented the air. Even in human form, the multitude of extra sensors on his tongue allowed him to pick up more than what another paranormal could. While she didn't scent of a lie, she didn't smell as if she was telling the whole truth, either.

"And if I were to decide to carry our son?" Basques rubbed his palm over Dloben's shoulder as he asked, teasing his fingertip over his bonding scar. "Would you protect my son with your life?"

Even as Dloben fought down a tremble from feeling Basques's touch to the flesh that had become a new erogenous zone, he saw the way the female enforcer blanched, then flushed. She gritted her teeth. Her eyes narrowed. However, she didn't respond.

"I'll take that as a *no*," Master Krispin commented mildly, a cold gleam entering his blue eyes, making them appear as cold as ice. Folding his hands on his desk as he leaned forward, he claimed, "I will not have an enforcer working for me that will not protect the children of the coven." When Tabatha opened her mouth, her anger perfuming the area, Krispin narrowed his eyes and barked, "Regardless of the species they end up being."

With her face flushing and a growl in her voice, Tabatha demanded, "What are you saying?"

Master Krispin rose to his feet, his expression turning serene. "I mean that your specist ways were unknown to me before now. I will not have someone such as yourself as an enforcer." When Tabatha opened her mouth, Krispin stated, "Unless you are willing to go through a rehabilitation course?"

Scoffing, Tabatha glanced around the room at everyone. "Seriously?" She pinned her gaze on Pierce. "Even you are okay with this?"

Pierce shrugged. "Do I think the idea is freakier than shit . . . a dude giving birth? Sure." Smirking Dloben and Basques's way, he winked. "No offense."

"None taken," Dloben whispered on reflex.

Returning his attention to Tabatha, Pierce continued, "But children of any race are sacred. Who am I to judge?"

Tabatha crossed her arms over her chest and leaned back in her chair. "Fine," she muttered tartly. "I'll take a rehabilitation course. Better than losing my position."

Unable to keep his mouth shut, Dloben whispered, "She's lying." He ignored the way Tabatha's eyes widened in favor of adding, "She'll take the course, but she won't apply it." Cocking his head, he parsed out the other scents emanating from her. "She just needs to buy time to convince a couple more vampires to commit to a coup."

"You keep your mouth shut, abomination!" Tabatha shrieked as she leaped from her seat and lunged toward him.

Fear spiked through Dloben, and he cringed.

Crap! I really should have thought before speaking.

CHAPTER ELEVEN

Basques leaped to his feet, ready to tear Tabatha apart.
Tabatha had barely made it halfway across the large study
when Master Krispin intercepted her. Even having to round
the huge desk, he still managed to wrap his clawed hand
around the female vampire's neck. He lifted and shoved, tossing her back across the room.

Landing sprawled on the chair, Tabatha only remained fro-
zen for a second. She jumped back to her feet and hissed. Her
eyes hazed red, and her claws lengthened.

"You are weak," Tabatha snarled. "You won't last much
longer as coven master."

Instead of attacking Master Krispin, however, Tabatha
leaped toward the door. She had just managed to open it
when Krispin wrapped his hand around her upper arm and
spun her. He slammed her against the wall, grabbed both
wrists, and pinned them above her head with one hand, then
rested the claws of his other against Tabatha's throat. No matter how she wriggled, Tabatha couldn't escape the master
vampire's grip.

Krispin paused, petting her throat with his claws. While it
could have looked soothing, Basques knew better. It was a
threat and a promise. He could tear out her throat at any second.

"You seem to think I'm weak," Master Krispin commented
softly, his voice deadly serious. "Just because I didn't step in
to stop your ploy to birth a powerful male vampire, do not
mistake my patience for weakness."

Movement from the corner of his eye caught Basques's attention. He turned and spotted Dloben shaking on the sofa. Settling back into his seat, he wrapped his arms around his trembling beloved.

"Relax, beloved," Basques crooned into his ear.

"I-I'm sorry," Dloben mumbled, glancing around fearfully.

"For what?" Master Krispin asked the question.

Dloben pressed closer to Basques, but he answered. "I-I shouldn't have in-interfered."

Master Krispin cast a smile upon Dloben as he stated, "Your senses are far more acute than a vampire's, so while we could confirm that Tabatha hid something, we didn't catch the outright lie. You could." Waggling his brows, Krispin added, "Your abilities will be very useful, Dloben."

As Master Krispin turned back to Tabatha, Basques was pleased that Dloben's trembles eased off. "You're okay, handsome," Basques purred into his ear. "You did nothing wrong."

"You sure?" Dloben whispered back, peering up at him with wide, worried eyes. He darted his gaze toward the master, then returned his focus to Basques. "I don't want to get you into trouble by me speaking out of turn."

Basques pressed a hard kiss to Dloben's upturned lips. "The master appreciates honesty above all else." Then he smirked. "Well, except loyalty, but those two things go hand in hand for it to be true loyalty."

"O-Okay."

As Basques cuddled his still-uncertain lover to his chest, he turned his attention to the master.

"Are you gathering vampires to stage a coup, Tabatha?" Krispin kept his blunt questions restricted to *yes* or *no* answers.

"No," she replied sullenly, her gaze full of hate.

When everyone's attention turned to Dloben, his lover

tensed in his arms. Basques nuzzled his beloved's temple while whispering, "You're okay. Just tell them what you scent, handsome."

"She's telling the truth," Dloben mumbled, but he furrowed his brows. "There's something there, though. It's—" He paused and tipped his head, then his eyes widened. "Someone *else* is gathering the vampires, but she's part of it."

"How the fuck could he know that?" Pierce asked in a shocked voice.

Dloben hunched in on himself, and he glanced around at everyone. Basques could understand his trepidation. All the vampires in the room were staring at him in shock.

Basques had to admit that he was sort of curious himself. He had never before heard of a paranormal who could get that specific. His little beloved had some serious skills.

Sighing, Dloben focused on Tabatha. "I could explain . . . later."

Fortunately, Master Krispin nodded once, obviously understanding. Dloben didn't want to explain his abilities in front of someone who wasn't trustworthy.

"Of course." Master Krispin returned his focus to Tabatha. "Tabatha Solmon, you are hereby stripped of your position." Turning to stare at Second Ridger, he ordered, "Take her to the brig for now. We'll figure out the extent of her crimes soon enough."

"Yes, Master Krispin." Ridger rose to his feet and moved to take custody of Tabatha.

As soon as the master released Tabatha's wrist, she swiped. The master must have expected the move. He jerked beyond her reach, then lunged forward and slammed his claws into her side before yanking them free again.

Tabatha gasped and doubled over.

Second Ridger leaped onto her back and secured her arms

up with her hands behind her head. Tabatha howled, obviously in pain.

Master Krispin snorted. "Please," he sneered. "It's not a mortal wound. Calm yourself."

"Bastard," Tabatha raged, twisting in Second Ridger's grip. "You'll pay for this!"

"Not likely," Master Krispin commented mildly. "Have Doctor Ward check her after you've secured her in the cell."

Second Ridger nodded. "Yes, Master," he replied crisply, then turned and forced a straining Tabatha from the study.

Remembering what happened to Second Destrawn at the clutch, Basques ordered, "Enforcer Carmine, go watch his back."

While Master Krispin lifted a brow in obvious question, he didn't counter the order. After Carmine had disappeared from the room, Krispin closed the door. He pinned his gaze on Enforcer Pierce.

"Pierce, are you part of the coup being put together?"

Master Krispin's blunt question must have shocked Pierce, for the enforcer gaped for several heartbeats before snapping his mouth closed again. Then he shook his head vehemently. When Krispin responded by narrowing his eyes, Pierce glanced Dloben's way as his eyes widened.

"Oh, right." Pierce cleared his throat. "Sorry, Master. No, I have no knowledge of a coup against you." Then he growled low in his throat. "But I'll start being more mindful of any rumors that trickle to me."

Master Krispin peered at Dloben questioningly. "H-He's telling the truth." When the master nodded, Dloben tipped his head. His confusion perfumed the air. "Why do you believe my word over your peoples'?"

"We've been watching Tabatha for problems for quite some time," Master Krispin explained as he circled his desk and flopped into his chair. "Considering some of the other rumors we've heard about her plans, her involvement in a coup is not surprising at all."

Tracker Kraymer rose to his feet and crossed to the sideboard. "May I, Master?" he asked, pointing at the decanter of brandy.

The master smirked. "If you get a drink for all of us."

"Of course, Master." Kraymer glanced around at everyone. "Preferences?"

"Whiskey," Basques told him. He turned his attention to Dloben. "What about you, handsome?"

"Um." Dloben's brows furrowed. "I-I don't know. Never had any."

Basques hummed. "Okay." He drew the word out, then turned his attention to Kraymer. "Make him a mimosa." Smiling at Dloben, he told him, "Orange juice and champagne. If you don't like it, I'll drink it, and you can try something else."

"Okay."

Appreciating that his gargoyle acquiesced to him so easily, Basques squeezed his side once before decreasing his hold again. He relaxed in his seat as Kraymer made their drinks. Pierce wanted a brandy, and Krispin took a tumbler of tequila.

Basques realized no one had asked Kraymer directly just as he took the drink from him. "So. What about you, Kraymer?" he asked, pointedly stalling Dloben from taking a sip of the mimosa Kraymer had handed him. "You have a problem with my beloved?"

Kraymer grinned gamely. "My turn to be questioned, huh?" After Basques responded with a shrug, the tracker-in-training stated, "No. No, I don't have information on anyone organizing a coup, and I have no problem with gargoyles or even you possibly giving birth." Kraymer's expression clouded as he muttered, "In fact, I'm a little jealous. I know

I'm gay, and I never thought I'd get to have kids, but if I bond with a gargoyle, then there might still be a chance."

Dloben cocked his head. "Maybe you should find out if you can meet the rest of the gargoyles at the clutch manor," he commented absently. "There are dozens of unmated men there."

A low growl rumbled through Basques. "You're not going back there." Upon seeing the way Dloben's jaw sagged open, he quickly added, "Not until Chasis and Ducine are caught."

Just as quickly as the shocked scent filled the air, it was gone. Instead, Dloben beamed up at him. "Okay."

Relief that his heavy-handed manner didn't bother his beloved, Basques blew out a harsh breath. "Thank you." Then he dipped his head and sealed his lips over Dloben's own. For a moment, he took his time teasing his beloved's tongue and tasting his unique, wonderful flavor. When he broke the kiss, Basques rested his forehead against his gargoyle's. "You taste so damn delicious."

"Gods, I need to make a rule that only *I* am allowed to make out in my office," Master Krispin grumbled, but there wasn't any true heat in it. He took his tequila from Kraymer, smirking as he took a sip.

Basques smirked right back as he took a swallow of his own drink. As he watched, Dloben sipped his beverage. His gargoyle's features lip up, and he smiled as he took a healthier swallow.

"Good?" Basques couldn't help but ask, just so he could see Dloben focus his smile on him.

To Basques's pleasure, Dloben did just that. "Yes, tasty. Thanks."

After everyone had settled with their drinks, Master Krispin leaned back in his chair and kicked up his heels on his desk. "So, Dloben. Again, welcome to the coven."

Just as he often did, Dloben tensed at being called out. Fortunately, it was short-lived. After a couple of heartbeats, he relaxed into Basques's side.

"Thank you, Master Krispin," Dloben offered formally, his tone respectful.

"Now that we've confirmed that everyone here in my inner circle is trustworthy" — the master's expression turned curious — "how is it that you can figure out so many things from a vampire's words and scent?"

Sighing, Dloben rubbed his palm over Basques's thigh.

Probably a nervous habit.

In response, Basques nuzzled his temple with his lips and whispered, "Only if you're comfortable." He held his long-time friend's gaze as he murmured, "If you need more time to become familiar with us all, then it's okay to ask for that, too. There is no wrong answer here."

Master Krispin's lips twitched just a little, but he did dip his head a tiny smidge. The movement was enough for Basques to recognize that his master and friend realized the subject could be uncomfortable. It also told him that Krispin would accept his enforcer's word on the matter.

"N-No, it's okay," Dloben mumbled. As Basques watched, his cheeks took on a pinkish hue. After clearing his throat, Dloben explained, "Back at my clutch, the larger gargoyles ruled."

"When you say larger gargoyles, what do you mean?" That came from Pierce. The man had probably never seen a gargoyle before — of either size.

"Here. This is Chieftain Kinsey." Master Krispin pulled up a picture on his tablet, then handed it over to the third enforcer.

Well, second enforcer now, I guess.

"Damn. Big." Pierce focused on Basques. "And the one you tangled with was similar to this?"

Basques gave his underling a feral, toothy grin. "Yes. I

kicked Chasis's ass."

Pierce whistled before focusing on Dloben. "So there's big ones and small ones." His cheeks took on a pinkish hue, but he rallied and asked, "Can we see your true form?"

As odd as it sounded, Basques couldn't wait to see his gorgeous lover's swarthy blue skin once again. His lover's uniqueness was part of his draw. He turned his attention on Dloben.

Upon spotting Dloben's questioning expression, Basques nodded. "Go ahead, my beloved. You are welcome here." Nuzzling his nose along his man's neck, he rumbled, "And I love the way you look."

"Okay." Then Dloben sighed deeply and changed forms. As his skin rippled and his bones adjusted, his hands trembled.

Basques grabbed his mimosa glass, saving the beverage . . . more because he didn't want Dloben to be embarrassed. It only took a few seconds, then his gargoyle peered around the room from beneath his lashes. There was uncertainty in his scent, and he fidgeted just a little in his seat.

"Relax," Basques crooned, rubbing up and down his alternate arm. "You're safe. You're okay."

"Oh, wow," Pierce whispered.

Master Krispin hummed as he took in what the clothes didn't hide . . . which wasn't much. "Do you fly?"

"Yes, Master," Dloben replied, nodding. He rubbed his hand down his side as he glanced at his chest. "I have flaps of skin under my arms and attached to my sides. They're called wingskins." He twisted and pointed at the back of his ribcage, saying, "And I have bone-spurs that extend in several places on my ribcage to stretch them, which gives me the ability to fly."

Nodding, Master Krispin told him, "I would very much like to see that some time." Then he waved his hand in a *go ahead* gesture. "So, large and small gargoyles. Please, go on."

"Well, in most clutches, both gargoyles are treated the same." Dloben winced. "Or so I hear." Then he shook his head before adding, "Anyway, Chieftain Grecian favored the large and essentially used the small as slave labor."

Kraymer growled. "*Slave* labor? Like it sounds?"

Basques was reminded of just how young Kraymer was, considering all his interruptions. Still, he was a good vampire, learning quickly. Plus, he was top of his class and damn near as good as the coven's head tracker, Felistria.

Dloben nodded. "Yeah. Um, anyway" — he cleared his throat, obviously trying to move on quickly — "if we did something wrong, we were severely punished."

Then he growled and took his mimosa. He drained it in three gulps.

Kraymer bounced up and grabbed the empty glass to get him a refill.

Dloben kept talking. "There were some who liked to punish even if the job was done right, so they started giving orders in an obtuse manner. When we didn't get it exact, we were punished." He took the glass back from Kraymer and sipped it. "Whipping was a favorite."

"Relax, my beloved," Basques purred into his ear. "You're fine. You're safe." He gently grabbed his lover's nape and teased his mating mark. Knowing the sensitive bit of flesh would cause delicious tingles to sweep through his bonded love, Basques whispered, "Everyone here is a friend. Just relax."

To Basques's surprise, Dloben moaned before grumbling, "How am I supposed to relax when you do that?"

Basques chuckled softly, but he did stop rubbing over the claiming scar. "Just trying to relax you."

Dloben scowled at him. "*Not* relaxing."

Master Krispin barked a laugh. "Stop teasing your beloved

in my office so we can finish."

Rolling his eyes, Basques scowled at his master. Of course, he made certain his lover couldn't see, too. In response, Krispin offered a wide smile full of fangs.

Good thing Dloben was taking a sip of his drink at the time.

Dloben cleared his throat, his gaze darting around the room. "When you have to parse out every nuance of someone's words, tone, and scent, you begin to figure out how to read between the lines." He nibbled his bottom lip. After a sigh, Dloben whispered, "Look, it's not an exact science, but I've learned to be damn close when it comes to figuring out the truth of what's actually not said." Snuggling close to Basques, he whispered, "Otherwise, I never would have figured out how to do exactly what the enforcers ordered even when they didn't order it."

Basques allowed an angry growl to roll through his throat. "Damn them."

Gripping his wrist, Dloben told him, "Stop. The chieftain is dead, and the others scattered." Wincing, he whispered, "Even the second's own human mate, Kinsey's mother, won't have anything to do with him. He won't be long for this world."

"Good," Basques snarled, not at all sympathetic about a guy whose own beloved would turn against him. He would have had to do something damn horrible to have his own fated mate walk away from him.

Dloben snuggled against him as he took another sip of his mimosa. "Anyway, it made me really good at reading between the lines."

Basques vowed that not only would he never allow his relationship to deteriorate like that, but he would never see his beloved hurt that way again.

"Damn, that's a valuable skill," Pierce commented as he stared at Dloben in wonder.

Before Basques could come up with a response, Master Krispin's phone rang. "Hang on." A second later, he growled as he listened to whoever was on the phone. His gaze snapped to Basques and Dloben as he hung up. "We have a problem."

CHAPTER TWELVE

Dloben cringed. "Don't tell me someone attacked Second Ridger and Carmine, freeing Tabatha and escaping the clutch, um, coven." As soon as he finished blurting out all that, he slapped his hand over his mouth.

Master Krispin arched his left brow even as the corner of one lip curved up. Instead of annoyed, the expression appeared amused. He even shook his head.

"No, that was Chieftain Kinsey. He wanted to warn me that Chasis managed to escape. They're pressuring Ducine for information, but it's beginning to look as if he really doesn't know where the pal he rescued went." Master Krispin's eyes narrowed as he took a sip of his drink. Then he gave them both an enquiring look. "Do you really think an unbonded gargoyle could manage to come here" — he waved his hand vacantly, indicating their residence — "to try to retaliate for . . . whatever he's hung up on?"

Dloben finished his own drink, then sighed deeply. "I wish I could say no, but there's a definite possibility since he's a little . . . obsessed."

"Are you that good in bed?" Pierce asked, his tone clearly teasing. He even waggled his brows as he asked Basques, "Steal another guy's hot lover, and now he's after you?"

As Basques snarled, glaring angrily at Pierce, Dloben quickly shook his head. "No, I never slept with him." He even gripped his vampire's thigh and arm to keep him seated.

Basques relented, saying, "He's the asshole who left these bruises on my handsome beloved." Curving his lips in a feral smile, he said on a growl, "If he comes, I want him."

While Pierce raised his hands in surrender, a blush staining his cheeks, Master Krispin stated, "We will increase camera security for the roof and the surrounding areas." He leveled a reassuring smile Dloben's way. "You are one of mine now, Dloben, and I take care of my own." Then he grinned broadly. "Besides, how am I going to take complete advantage of your kickass truth-sensing skills if something happens to you?"

Some of Dloben's tension slipped away as a sense of security he hadn't ever felt before filled him. He hadn't felt that way when Chieftain Kinsey took over. Even when he'd bonded with Basques, it hadn't felt quite the same, either.

Dloben realized it had to be the combination—a lover of his own devoted to his happiness and a home where his safety was assured by Master Krispin. Plus, he could still garden, and he had a unique skill the coven master appreciated.

"Thank you, Master Krispin," Dloben replied, smiling tentatively at the male. "I'm happy to help any way I can."

"Good." Master Krispin rose to his feet, so everyone else in the room did the same. "Although I hear you favor working in the garden." As the master motioned toward the door, indicating a dismissal, he added, "You are welcome to do that, too."

Safe in Basques's arms, Dloben nodded happily.

Master Krispin patted Basques on his shoulder as he passed, saying, "Take a week to enjoy getting to know your beloved."

Basques nodded, grinning, clearly pleased. "Will do." Then he sobered. "But please keep me posted, Master."

Grinning, showing off his fangs, the master waggled his eyebrows. "Will do," he repeated, a hard edge sliding into his voice.

Moving his hand to Dloben's lower back, Basques escorted him out of the room. He used subtle pressure to indicate that he needed to turn left. As Dloben headed down the hall, those behind him hollered *congratulations, nice to meet yous,* and *welcome to the covens.*

Dloben felt warmed by their words. He sure hoped Tabatha's opinion ended up being in the minority. As Dloben thought about that, he realized he'd never actually discussed children with Basques . . . or how to control the process.

Shit!

When they stopped at a door and Basques started punching buttons on a panel, Dloben nibbled his bottom lip. "Lift your hand, Dloben," Basques ordered softly. "And stop looking so concerned. Nothing you say will make me walk away from you. You're everything to me." As Basques guided Dloben's hand to the panel, he added, "Now you'll be able to open and close the door to our quarters." Once he'd released his hand, Basques swept his gaze up and down Dloben's form, and his brows furrowed. "Maybe we should do it again in your human form."

Dloben nodded, happy for the delay, no matter what Basques had said. He shifted to his human form, then lifted his hand again. Once that was done, Dloben followed Basques into the suite.

As soon as the door closed, Dloben spun to face his lover and blurted out, "You might be pregnant!"

Basques cocked his head, his jaw sagging open. Releasing the knob, he licked his lips. He lifted his hands, and Dloben winced.

Seeing the pained expression on Basques's face, Dloben quickly muttered, "Sorry."

"And we're back there again," Basques said on a sigh before resting his hands on Dloben's shoulders. "How about you return to your true form, then tell me why you're sorry this time? Then explain why you think I could already be pregnant."

Dloben changed forms again. With all the practice he'd

been getting in the last day, he was getting pretty good at it. He also felt fortunate that due to his small frame in either form, he still fit in the same clothes.

He'd seen some of the larger gargoyles bust seams when returning to gargoyle form while fully clothed.

As soon as Dloben finished, Basques slid his hands down his arms and, stepping close, wrapped them around his torso. He pulled him flush to his chest, then dipped his head. Sealing his mouth over Dloben's, Basques slid his tongue out and pushed his way past his lips.

Moaning softly, Dloben opened, only too happy to give in to his lover's demands. He clutched at the sides of his big vampire's torso and pressed against him. While he tangled his tongue with Basques's, his blood fired through his veins, flooding his groin.

Dloben rocked his hips, searching for friction to his hard dick. Feeling Basques slot his legs between his own and press his thigh against his trapped erection, he groaned into his vampire's mouth. Unable to help himself — being held in Basques's arms and ravished just felt too good — Dloben began rocking.

Popping his hips forward in hard thrusts, Dloben felt his brain go offline. Blood rushed through his ears. His body trembled. His cock throbbed and jerked, and his balls tingled.

The house could have been burning around him, and Dloben wouldn't have noticed. All that mattered was the delicious sensations Basques created within him . . . and getting more of them.

Oh, and the thick rod pressing into his stomach. That mattered, too. He reveled in the knowledge that he did that to his vampire.

Finally, Basques lifted his head, breaking the kiss. Immediately a long, low moan erupted from Dloben's throat. He tightened his hold on his vampire's body, and when Basques lowered his head and lapped across his neck, a full-body shudder worked through him.

Sweat beaded on his temples, and a fresh wash of need surged through him.

"P-Please," Dloben hissed roughly, his body twitching almost spastically. "I-I need."

"Then come, my sweet gargoyle," Basques snarled gruffly. At the same time, he pressed his thigh upward, increasing the pressure on Dloben's balls. "Now."

Dloben could do nothing but obey. His balls pulled tight, and his seed pulsed from him in body-jolting spirts. Tipping his head back, Dloben roared his bliss as his senses reeled.

Just as Dloben began to settle back into himself, realizing Basques was the only reason he was still standing, he felt his vampire sink his teeth into his neck. His body jolted again as a new wave of ecstasy sang through his veins. His cock thickened anew, and he unloaded in his jeans a second time.

Basques moaned, the sound vibrating his neck.

As each sucking pull on Dloben's neck went straight to his twitching dick, he vaguely acknowledged Basques's strangled moan, and the big male's arms tightened just that much more. The vampire's hips jerked, pressing his dick against Dloben's stomach rhythmically, betraying that he had found his pleasure. The smell of his salty goodness filling the air also gave it away.

When Basques eased his fangs from Dloben's neck and licked along it, he hummed in Dloben's ear. "You are just too hard to resist, my beloved." He chuckled huskily. "Good thing I don't even need to try, right?"

Dloben tipped his head, allowing him to smile up at Basques from where he rested his cheek on his chest. "Definitely don't try. Love this." Scratching his claws over Basques's cloth-covered back, he mumbled, "Love you." Realizing what had slipped out, Dloben felt his cheeks heat, and he dipped his head.

"Oh, no," Basques stated on a growl. "Can't hide after saying something like that."

Basques adjusted his hold and swept Dloben into his arms. With a squeak, he clung to his vampire as the big man moved across the room. He settled onto a large chair, Dloben clutched on his lap.

Peering at Basques through his lashes, Dloben tried to gauge his lover's reaction. To his surprise, he saw that Basques was smiling at him.

Huh.

His vampire cradled his jaw and pecked a chaste kiss to his lips.

"So, you love me?" Basques crooned, nuzzling his temple against Dloben's own.

If he'd been a shifter, Dloben would have thought the man was marking him with his scent. Did vampires do that, too? He realized they still had so much to talk about.

Later, though.

"Yes," Dloben whispered. He wouldn't, couldn't, lie to his mate. "I love you." After clearing his throat, he murmured, "I know you're not supposed to say it during sex"—his cheeks began to warm, and he knew he blushed—"or directly after, and it's okay if you don't feel the same, but it is true, and—"

"Easy, beloved," Basques purred, pressing the pads of his forefingers to Dloben's lips, ceasing his ramblings. "It's good that you love me, Dloben." His deep blue eyes twinkled with his happiness. "Because I love you, too."

Dloben gasped. "Really?"

Basques nodded.

"Why?" Dloben winced, but all Basques did was laugh.

Clutching him close, Basques pecked a kiss to Dloben's lips before grinning down at him. "You're my beloved, Dloben. The other half of my soul." Winking, he asked, "Why do you love me?"

"I—" Dloben wasn't certain how to answer that. Cocking his head, he admitted, "I just do." Realizing how lame that sounded, he hurried to add, "You hold me. You're patient with me. You don't mind that I'm uneducated or uncertain about things." Then, gathering his courage, Dloben purred, "You love my trilling, and you're hot as hell."

Basques growled. "All those things right back atcha and more." Then he sealed his lips over Dloben's again, and his hands began roving over Dloben's body.

Dloben decided to do a little exploring of his own. As he pushed into the kiss, he shoved his hands under Basques's shirt. Rucking it up, he traced over the lines of the big vampire's abdominals. Then Dloben slid his hands up and teased at his nipples, plucking and rolling the hardened nubs.

Groaning, Basques shifted in his seat as he broke the kiss. "Damn it. I already have a crotch full of cum." Barking a laugh, he stated, "Getting off in our clothes is becoming a habit. How about we go take a shower?"

Dloben opened his mouth to agree, but what came out was something totally different. "Will you still love me if you're pregnant?"

"Yes," Basques replied without hesitation. Scraping his fingernails through Dloben's hair, he urged, "Maybe you should tell me why you feel that way?"

Sighing, Dloben knew he had to come clean. "Well." He rubbed his palms over Basques's chest absently as he told him, "Because we've had a lot of sex over the last couple of days, and we haven't eaten any cinnamon."

"Cinnamon?" Basques's eyebrows lifted. "So, if I eat cinnamon and you fuck me, that's a contraceptive?"

Dloben nodded.

Basques massaged Dloben's scalp as he gave him a reassuring smile. "Well, to be fair, you've only fucked me the one time while we were bonding." He gave Dloben a lascivious once-over. "The rest of the time, it's been my dick in your sweet, hot ass."

"Once might have been enough," Dloben pointed out.

"Might have been, and if that happens, it happens." Basques shrugged. "While my choice would have been to wait until we're a bit more settled with each other, having a gorgeous gargoyle child with you certainly won't be a hardship." Basques chuckled as he traced his fingers along Dloben's brow ridges. "Maybe he'll have these sexy, unique, vertically slitted pupils like you. Gods, your pale green eyes are gorgeous."

Gaping, Dloben stared in surprise for a few seconds. "You think they're gorgeous?"

"Most definitely." Then Basques levered to his feet, but he didn't put Dloben down. "I'll give you a tour later. Right now, my groin itches, and I'm sure yours does, too." Snorting, Basques started through the space. "I can't wait to get you all naked and soapy in my shower. I feel the need to sink into you again."

Dloben's gut clenched, and his arousal soared anew. "B-But what about, um, p-pregnant?"

Basques shrugged one shoulder. "How long until we'd know?"

Racking his brain, Dloben tried to remember what his parents had told him about sex-ed so many decades before. "Um . . . I don't know," he admitted. "I'll have to call Doctor Cantral."

"Okay," Basques replied, sounding so comfortable with everything they'd discussed. "Then after the shower, that's what we'll do."

Dloben, on the other hand, was nonplussed. "How can you be so relaxed about this?"

Basques crossed a large bedroom, making his way into a gorgeous ensuite. "Dloben, we'll handle everything as it comes." After putting him back on his feet, Basques cradled his face in his hands and peered down at him, his love gleaming in his deep blue eyes. "We're a team and can handle whatever happens as long as we stick together."

"Okay," Dloben whispered, more than on board with that.

"So, whether it's a baby or facing off with Chasis or building our new home here together," Basques told him, whispering the words in his ear as he nuzzled their cheeks together. "We do it all . . . together."

"Together," Dloben whispered, holding tight to his vampire. "Always."

"Yesss . . . now get in here." Basques chuckled huskily. "I want more *together time*."

Dloben giggled as Basques quickly stripped him, then dragged him into the shower. He was more than on board with more together time with the vampire who'd changed his life . . . in the best way possible.

YOU MAY ALSO ENJOY THE FOLLOWING FROM EXTASY BOOKS INC:

Pack, Strap, Carry
Charlie Richards

Excerpt

Patrick Dolcet kept the smile pasted on his face even though he would much rather have glared at his belligerent date. This was the last time he would agree to a blind date from one of the partners at his firm. One way or another, Patrick would find a way out of it.

Maybe that's what I'll do when I get home . . . think up a list of acceptable excuses.

"So, I was thinking we could skip dessert," Walter stated. Resting his forearms on the table, he leaned toward Patrick and leered at him. "I'd much rather we head to my hotel room and fuck." Walter hummed as he perused Patrick's body — what he could see of it anyway. "I want to sink my dick in your tight ass so damn bad. You ready to go?"

Good grief. The nerve of this guy!

So shocked, Patrick had to clear his throat before finding his voice. "Uh, as flattering as that is, I'm sorry, Walter. I have a meeting with a client tomorrow morning, and there's still a few things I need to get together." He did his best to keep his tone even, not allowing the disgust he felt to bleed through.

Walter snorted as he shook his head. "I don't want to sleep with you. I just want to fuck you." He lifted his hand, obviously attempting to get the waitress's attention. "There'll still be plenty of time for you to do that after I fill your ass."

The arrival of the waitress gave Patrick a second to think. "Hey, gentlemen. Can I interest you in some coffee or dessert?" she asked with a perky smile.

Gentlemen. Ha! If she only knew.

"No, thanks," Walter replied. "Just the check."

"Of course," she replied before turning away and heading off.

Walter stood, saying, "While you take care of that, I'm gonna go piss. Be right back."

Patrick watched in silence as Walter walked toward the back of the restaurant. As soon as his date was out of sight, relief flooded him. He pulled out his wallet.

As much as it galled Patrick to pay for Walter's dinner without a fight, it was just the break he needed. He slid a pen and the receipt from his cab ride to the restaurant from the inside of his suit coat pocket. On the back of the slip of paper, Patrick wrote a quick note.

I received an emergency call from a client. The dinner is paid for. Have a good night.

Patrick left the note on Walter's empty plate, then returned the pen to his pocket. Without waiting for the check, he pulled his wallet out. He had a good idea of how much the dinner had cost, so he left ample cash on the table.

Then Patrick swiftly exited the restaurant.

Crossing the sidewalk to the street, Patrick glanced up and down the road. He spotted a taxi in the distance and stuck out his arm to flag it down. To his relief, the taxi stopped, and he quickly climbed inside.

After giving the cabbie his address, Patrick relaxed back in the seat and heaved a grateful sigh.

"Long day, sir?" the cabbie asked, glancing at him in the

rearview mirror.

Patrick focused on the man. "No," he replied with a shake of his head. "A bad date."

The cabbie's expression turned commiserating. "I remember those. Never been more grateful than when I found my wife." The man's smile became one of fondness. "Now I don't have to worry about that anymore."

Upon recognizing the look of adoration on the man's face as he spoke of the woman who was obviously the love of his life, Patrick felt a pang of something in the vicinity of his heart. He wished someone would feel that way about him. Unfortunately, so far, all his attempts at relationships had failed miserably.

Thirty-one years old, and the longest relationship I've managed is four months.

That had been with a firefighter named Trace, and they'd ended amicably. The relationship had just sort of . . . fizzled. They were even still friends. In fact, Trace was the one who'd given his card to the client he had to see in the morning.

Once again, Patrick had to force a smile. "I'm happy for you."

The cabbie must have read something in his tone, for he gave him a reassuring smile. "You'll find her, son. Have faith."

Patrick couldn't remember the last time someone hadn't taken one look at him and jumped to the conclusion that he was gay. Hell, he not only wore lip gloss but eyeliner as well. Of course, it could have been because the cabbie was more focused on the road.

"Him," Patrick corrected softly. "And I sure hope so." This time, Patrick didn't have to force his smile. "It'd be really nice to have someone to come home to after a long day."

Without missing a beat, the cabbie replied, "Find him, then. If a relationship is what you want, never stop looking." He grinned as he used his rearview mirror to meet Patrick's gaze for an instant before returning his focus to the road. "There's a soul mate out there for everyone."

Nodding, Patrick prayed the man was right.

The trill of Patrick's phone caught his attention. He pulled it out and grimaced. Having no desire to talk to Walter, he denied the call, sending it to voicemail.

A moment later, his phone beeped, indicating Patrick had a message. Patrick pressed a button and lifted the phone to his ear. Walter's angry voice came through the line.

"You just think you're gonna cut and run on me, man? I was promised you'd put out. I can't wait to tell Freedman you made a liar out of him." Walter's voice lowered to a nasty snarl as he added, "I also think I'm gonna start a few rumors unless you're at my hotel in thirty minutes. Get your ass over here, or you'll be sorry."

Patrick was already sorry . . . sorry he'd allowed Richard Freedman to talk him into a date with Walter. While the man was a senior partner, Patrick should have known better. He should never have decided to do a little brown nosing.

When the cabbie came to a stop before Patrick's small home, he pulled out his wallet and gave the man a nice tip. He climbed out and headed up the walk. By the time he'd walked into his home, Patrick had decided on his course of action.

Leaving his keys on the hook by the door, Patrick headed to the kitchen. He grabbed a tumbler, then added a couple of ice cubes. When Patrick reached the sideboard, he filled his glass with spiced rum.

Patrick took a sip as he crossed to his sofa. The beverage caused his tongue to tingle, and his taste buds sang pleasantly. After swallowing the mouthful, Patrick set his tumbler on the coffee table so he could remove his jacket.

After draping his suit jacket over the back of the sofa, Patrick picked up the handset phone from the end table. It had been on his to do list forever to get rid of the landline, but he'd been too busy . . . or too lazy. There always seemed to be something more important than making a call to a phone center and dealing with a pushy sales representative.

Now it's a good thing.

Patrick dialed Richard's number. While he didn't consider the man a friend, not really, he'd collaborated with him on cases enough times that he felt comfortable ringing him at nine-thirty at night. As he waited for Richard to answer his call, Patrick picked up his drink and settled in his recliner.

"Hey, Patrick," Richard offered by way of greeting. "Everything going okay? Calling to thank me?"

As if.

"Hi, Richard." Patrick hesitated just a second, then told the other man, "Afraid not. Walter and I didn't hit it off. Not my type, but I was going to ask you how well you knew the man."

"Not exceptionally well," Richard admitted. "I met him at a conference three years ago. He hit on me, and I told him I wasn't gay." Chuckling softly, he admitted, "Flattering, but even if I was bisexual, he wouldn't be my type. I like my partners with some weight to them."

That was probably more than Patrick needed to know about Richard's sex life but whatever.

Before Patrick could respond, Richard asked, "Why do you ask?"

"Well, he made a number of inappropriate comments and expected me to let him fuck me," Patrick stated, deciding to be blunt. "When I attempted to politely decline, he pushed the issue, so I left. Then he left a message on my phone that could be taken as threatening."

For several long seconds, no sound came through the line. Patrick even pulled his phone away from his ear to be certain he hadn't dropped the call. The timer still ticked away.

Finally, his voice low and quiet, Richard stated, "He can definitely be an ass, but are you sure about being threatened? Could you have misunderstood?"

Patrick wasn't surprised that Richard didn't want to believe ill of his friend. "Well, take a listen to this, and tell me what you think." He was glad he'd saved Walter's message. As Patrick pulled it up on his cell phone, he commented, "You can tell me if it's all bluster."

The sound of Walter's voice filled the air, and Patrick hoped it would carry through the line. When the belligerent man finished speaking, silence fell again. Patrick waited . . . impatiently.

Finally, Richard's deep sigh came through the line. "Yeah, that . . ." He sighed again. "I didn't tell him you'd have sex with him. I'd mentioned your name a few times over the years, and he wanted to meet you."

"Well, we met," Patrick replied dryly. He scoffed as he thought about his evening. "I just thought you should know how it turned out. That way if he calls—" Patrick paused, uncertain how to explain his aversion to the asshole without sounding like a judgmental ass himself.

"I get it," Richard murmured. "If he calls, I'll deal with it."

"I appreciate it," Patrick replied, a wave of relief washing over him. "Sorry to interrupt your night."

"No, it's fine. This'll teach me to never play matchmaker," Richard grumbled. "Not ever again."

Patrick laughed. He knew that feeling all too well. Realizing he didn't have anything else to say, Patrick cleared his throat. "Well, I think I'm gonna enjoy this rum, take a shower, and review some case files."

"Sounds like an exciting evening," Richard replied. "Good night."

"Night." Then Patrick disconnected the line and set both phones on the coffee table.

Patrick did exactly as he'd told the other man, and when he received another call from Walter, he silenced his phone and ignored the message.

I'll deal with it tomorrow.

ABOUT THE AUTHOR

Charlie started writing fantasy when she was eight, and after stumbling onto her first erotic romance at age nineteen, she realized her true calling. She now focuses on writing gay erotic romance, normally of the paranormal variety, with heroes of all kinds. With the help and support of her husband, Charlie finally fulfilled one of her life-long goals . . . move to acreage with her horses. You can often find her curled up with her laptop and a cup of tea or glass of wine, creating her next adventure. Charlie enjoys exploring the mountains of her new Oregon home on horseback, 4-wheeler, or motorcycle.

She can be reached at ch.richards2010@yahoo.com
Or visit her at www.charlie-richards.com

www.ingramcontent.com/pod-product-compliance
Lightning Source LLC
Chambersburg PA
CBHW060639130626
46555CB00002B/867